# Death
# &
# The Seagull

## Mark Feakins

**Books by Mark Feakins**

**The Rye Series:**
#1 The Rye Rooftop Club
#2 The Rye Rooftop Club: Mother's Day

Death & The Seagull

## Note From The Author

There are very few novels set in Bexhill-On-Sea, but the most famous is Agatha Christie's ABC Murders, published in 1936.

For lovers of mysteries and puzzles, I have hidden a reference to Mrs Christie's book within this story as a tribute.

Happy hunting and you will find the answer at the end of the book.

*For Kevin and Rebecca Gordon.*
*Friends forever, wherever we are.*

# PROLOGUE

Monday, I received two letters.

Tuesday, I became a father.

Wednesday, I was on the run.

Thursday, I fell to my death.

Friday, I caught my killer.

It was quite a week.

# CHAPTER 1

Ever since I was a young boy, I have been unable to resist the lure of a good café. Bars and restaurants are all very well, but the humble café has an attraction all of its own. The best of them have just the right combination of ingredients – the soft décor complimenting not distracting from the food, the aroma of coffee and fresh baking suspended in the air, a display of scones and cakes that requires unhurried consideration, friendly staff whose plumpness suggests the food is just too good to resist.

During my first visit, only thirty minutes before, Café Amato had appeared to have all these ingredients in abundance, with the added bonus of being located beside the sea that sparkled in the summer sun. But everything had changed. Nothing was the same; crockery crashed, forks scraped, the blue and white décor clashed, the sun blinded.

If only I hadn't fired the gun.

The noise had been deafening. The explosion, thunderous. My ears rang and my hand shook. It hadn't been my fault. He surprised me, lunging like that. I hadn't come to Bexhill to shoot anyone. I'd come because Hazel had asked me. Long dead, Hazel, my childhood friend.

This wasn't how things were meant to go.

Looking for something positive to steady myself, I put my teacup back on its saucer as gently as I could with shaking hands and reached for my notebook. The little leather book contained my lists and always lived in my trouser pocket, ready to provide structure and comfort when required. I like a list. I'm the kind of man who feels much better with a list. So, I pulled the stubby pencil from its spine and turned to a fresh page. *List of Events Leading up to the Unfortunate Shooting Incident* I wrote across the top; the letters untidy from my unsteady hand. In order to try and make sense of it all, I began to list the key events that had brought me to this awful moment:

*1. Monday, received two letters.*

Monday rarely brought any interesting post, but two letters had shot through my letter box with a clatter and they had changed everything. Had it only been yesterday?

One letter told me that I must report to the hospital in a week's time to begin my treatment. Treatment I knew would be both undignified and useless. I would still die, the harassed doctor, with spectacles that jittered as she spoke, knew that as well as I did. She made all the right noises about being able to slow things down, hold things up, buy some time, but we both knew that the offer was kind, but futile. So, I had to decide before next Monday whether to begin the treatment or simply depart this world with grace in the next few months at a time of nature's choosing. Not unhappily, as I have found it very difficult to go on without Maggie. She was my wife and she was marvellous. She brought such joy to life. To my life. I miss her.

So, I set Friday as my decision day, or D-Day as I had

christened it. I had to decide whether to undergo the treatment or just let my body's failures take their course. This would allow me enough time to cancel all work for the foreseeable future, empty the fridge, iron my best pyjamas and prepare a bag of other hospital essentials. Or, send a polite note explaining that I had chosen not to attend the hospital, but thanking them for their assistance to date.

The second letter had been forwarded from my mother's address, her erratic writing scrawled across the top and down the side, *'Redirect this to my son, Howard, please, he left home a long time ago.'*. It turned out to be from an old friend who I had not seen since we were eighteen, more than thirty years ago. She had vanished overnight, and no one seemed to know where she had gone. The letter explained it all, why she had disappeared so suddenly, where she had been and that she was, at the time of writing, facing the same fate I now faced.

I had sat at my kitchen table for what must have been more than twenty minutes, just looking at Hazel's writing. The letter had taken seventeen years to reach me. She must now be long dead, but the surprises didn't stop there. The letter contained even more staggering news, life changing perhaps, if my life hadn't already changed beyond all recognition. Hazel was asking me to undertake a delicate mission, her final request she called it. I knew I must act quickly in order to be back for Friday's D-Day.

*2. Bexhill-On-Sea*

I live in Brighton and it's a short, pleasant train ride through the Sussex Downs to Bexhill-On-Sea, the site of my mission, as outlined by Hazel. I arrived late Monday evening and settled into the Sunnyside Guest House, a pleasant place of oak panels and cheery floral swags. I used Tuesday morning to get the lay of the land, walk the busy promenade and locate the Marina Garage, where I was to return at the end of the day to fulfil Hazel's last wish.

### 3. Tuesday, solicitor

My solicitor, used by my father and so in turn by me, was based in Bexhill, having relocated from my home town of Rye when Old Mr Moon was replaced by his son, Young Mr Moon. I took the opportunity to pop in and ensure that everything was prepared, having begun to put my affairs in order over the last week or so. It had been my first face to face meeting with Young Mr Moon, who introduced himself as Simon or Si, apparently either would do. I settled on Simon. He complimented me on my efficiency and the comprehensive list of items to be arranged I had sent to him, and he had reassured me that everything was in hand.

### 4. Late lunch

Calculating that there would be fewer interruptions towards the end of the afternoon I had decided to call in to The Marina Garage at 4pm, so I treated myself to a late lunch. Café Amato was both a convenient location, being just around the corner from the garage, and held an envious position on the seafront with views past the imposing Art Deco triumph that is the De La Warr Pavilion to the sea beyond.

I had met the owner, Mrs A, a pleasingly plump woman who turned out to be an excellent baker. Her round, rich cheese scones proving to be just as triumphant as the neighbouring architecture.

## 5. The Seagull at the garage

I remembered a seagull laughing its loud *huah-huah* above me as I stood in front of The Marina Garage an hour or so later. It was not what I had expected. It was little more than a dilapidated old shed, not the ideal place for the delicate matter that I was bringing to its flaking wooden doors. My tummy was suddenly full of nerves, fighting for space with the two cheese scones I had recently consumed. Looking back, it could have been some sort of premonition of all that was about to befall me, but I simply took it as a sign of the scale of the news I was about to impart to the stranger within. I was about to change her life forever. I wished Maggie had been with me, leading the charge. She'd have known what to do and say.

As I stood hesitating, the seagull circling in the blue sky above, the sun was beginning to roast the top of my head and I could feel the sweat rife inside my suit. I could wait no longer, so, I wiped the dampness from my forehead with my cotton hanky, hauled my belt up under my stomach and crossed the yard toward the battered wooden building. I slipped inside, not pausing to knock, fearing any sort of hiatus might give me an excuse to turn tail and retreat.

## 6. The Gun!

As my eyes adjusted from the bright sunlight outside to the gloom of the interior, I was met with my first ever sighting of a gun. Other than in films and television programmes, I had lived my fifty years without ever seeing any sort of firearm, and yet here it was. A gun, held in the hand of a thin man with appalling posture, who was pointing it at an overall-clad young woman cowering in the corner.

She shook her head at him, "This is crazy," she said.

"Just give it back," he said, in a surprisingly pleasant voice.

The young woman frowned, more in frustration than fear it seemed, "I don't have anything. I brought back what you gave me."

"Don't be stupid," said the man with the beginnings of a hump. "Everything is counted. Do you think we're stupid?" My stomach lurched as he took a step towards her, the gun aimed directly between her eyes.

"Please," she said. "Don't make me hurt you." Which I thought was plucky in her present situation.

He snorted, "Becky, Becky, you've got it all mixed up. You're the one about to get..."

As he took another menacing step, out of the blue the girl's left hand swung in a wide arc and the large spanner it held cracked across his wrist. He yelped and twisted to his left as the gun flew through the air, bounced off the closed door and spun across the ground. He recovered quickly and turned back, managing to block the spanner before it struck him for a second time. As if from nowhere, his other hand produced a vicious looking knife and he pinned her against the workbench, tools and car parts scattering in all directions.

"Why did you have to do that? We were just going to talk," he panted, the knife perilously close to her throat. "Tell me where it is or I'm going to rearrange this sweet little face of yours, so even your Daddy wouldn't recognise you."

Suddenly, a third voice joined the fray, "Please don't say that. I wouldn't want to fire this gun, but I'm afraid I might have to."

All three of us froze, as I imagine we were all a little shocked. In the brief pause that followed it dawned on me that the voice had been mine. Although I had no memory of doing so, it seemed I had retrieved the weapon from where it had landed near my feet, and was now pointing it at the rounded shoulders of the gunman's back. Maggie had always been the one in our marriage with more of the gung-ho about her, so this was quite an unexpected turn of events.

Becky's eyes, wide with surprise, slid over the shoulder of her attacker and locked on to mine. I attempted a brief smile by way of introduction, but quickly returned my focus to the knife being held tightly beneath her chin.

"Now," I managed to say, despite all moisture beating a hasty retreat from my mouth. "I suggest, with the greatest respect, that you step away from the young lady... slowly... oh, and perhaps you could raise your hands at the same time?"

The thin chap paused, obviously considering his options, unaware of whether I was a man used to handling a gun in situations such as this or simply a middle-aged upholsterer who badly needed the toilet. He clearly decided not to take the risk and raised his hands to the level of his shoulders and stepped backwards.

"Let's not do anything silly," he said.

"Shush, just turn around slowly and drop the knife. You can then sit quietly on the floor while we call the police," I said, with more confidence than I felt.

"No!" they chorused the moment the authorities were mentioned.

"There's no need for that," Becky said. "It's just a misunderstanding."

By now the attacker had turned around, his hands still in the air. He was in his mid-twenties and had a long face, with rather smart frameless glasses perched on his bony nose, "You see, no need to get excited."

"I can assure you that I am far from excited." I snapped back. "This is not at all how things were supposed to go when I planned them this morning."

"I can see this isn't your thing," he continued. "You've clearly never handled a gun before, the chances of you actually using it are non-existent. So, why don't we..."

I waved the gun towards him, "I have no idea why you would draw that conclusion. I have an excellent knowledge of... gunmanship."

He stifled a snigger, "Gunmanship? Let's not mess about, you don't even have your finger on the trigger."

As he said this, three things happened simultaneously:

1. I looked at my fingers and saw that he was right.

2. He took a step towards me.

3. Wagner's The Ride of The Valkyries started to play loudly from the phone in my jacket pocket.

The result of these three individual actions was that I put my finger on the trigger just as the music started and he made his move. Naturally, I tensed with fear and surprise, which lead to an almighty bang echoing around the garage and the gun recoiling with a violent twitch.

Becky screamed and turned away as the thin man flew backwards and bounced off the Fiat Panda that stood quietly in the middle of the room. My ears rang from the sound of the shot as the music in my pocket ceased and I stared down at his body, still and silent with glasses askew and blood leaking from his forehead. My knees felt weak and I began to sink to the floor.

"No, no," Becky shouted, quite forcefully, I thought. "Don't faint, don't!"

She dashed towards me, grabbed me under the arms and hauled me to my feet, before taking the gun from my hand and rubbing it vigorously with a greasy rag taken from her overall pocket.

"You must never mention this again," she said. "If you say anything, it'll be *you* the police'll be after. I'll clean your prints off the gun and sort everything, do you understand?"

Before I could form a reply, she had pushed me firmly out of the garage doors, which I heard her lock behind me.

## 7. The Giant

I stood back in the concrete yard, my legs continuing to tremble and the sunlight stinging my eyes. Before I had time to gather my thoughts, I heard the sound of heavy footsteps and a great deal of wheezing coming up the drive.

"Carl? Are you okay?" a deep, breathy voice called.

I peered around the corner to see an enormous man with extensive facial hair lumbering towards me. I turned back to the shed and tried to open the door, but it was firmly locked. I looked around me. The rickety garage was tight against a wall to my left, but to my right there appeared to be a pathway at the end of the building. I quickly made my way to it and disappeared around the corner, just as the wheezing giant entered the yard.

The path led to the back of the garage and, as I moved along between it and the high brick wall, the giant started hammering on the flimsy wooden doors behind me, "Carl? Carl, speak to me. What's happened?"

Suddenly, Becky shot out of a small door ahead of me, a rucksack on her back, and disappeared through a gap in the wall. I breathed a sigh of relief to see that there was a way out and quickly followed her into an alley between the rows of houses. I looked left and right but she was nowhere to be seen. Behind me a strained voice floated through the back door of the garage, "Slim, get in here. I'm bleeding. She's gone. And call Ellis. Call Ellis, NOW!"

The thin chap, now identified as Carl, was alive. Thank goodness. Relief flooded through me. It was clear he was not a good person, but even so, I was pleased not to have killed him. As the giant, incongruously referred to as Slim, pounded on the front doors I picked up my pace and headed down the alleyway toward the seafront.

I hurried around the corner and spotted Café Amato in the distance. A desperate need for a cup of tea and a toilet overtook all other considerations and I practically ran towards its inviting blue and white exterior.

My thoughts matched my pounding steps; What to do? What to do? I'd just shot someone, albeit by mistake - but more importantly, I had shot him in front of the woman I believed to be my daughter.

# CHAPTER 2

My hands shook as I lifted the china cup to my lips and the tea sloshed sideways. I watched it crest the rim and run down my fingers, finding myself unable to do anything about it.

I was sitting in the same seat at the same table as my earlier visit, pretending to be a law-abiding citizen this time. How was this happening? I wasn't a person who fired guns, shot people, fled gangsters – I was an upholsterer. My upbringing had been in an environment made up of chaos and eccentricity, which had turned me into a man of order - spices alphabetised and racked, books in subject order and aligned, socks ironed and arranged by length of service. That's what I brought to the world – order. Maggie was always looking to me for organisational back-up. My ability to find things in her creative maelstrom had been honed to a fine art after growing up hunting down my mother's slippers in the fridge or her glasses in the biscuit tin.

I lay down my stubby pencil and re-read my list of events that outlined all that had happened. It all seemed so unbelievable. I took a faltering sip of tea, careful not to let the drips splash on my cream linen suit, which had been chosen in calmer times to make a good first impression. Well, that was out the window now. What should have been a tender moment had become one of confusion and slaughter. No, Carl wasn't actually dead, I reminded myself, I had heard him speak. So, it wasn't murder, just attempted murder perhaps... in self-defence? Or in error?

I carefully placed the teacup back on the saucer and forced myself to focus on wiping my unsteady hands on the paper serviette with a forget-me-not pattern. Then I turned the page of my little notebook and began a fresh list; *Positives from Unfortunate Shooting Incident.*

Well, the first positive was that I had met my daughter. Although, among the threats and gun smoke, I'm pretty sure she hadn't clocked that her father had entered her life through the garage's warped front doors. It was certainly not the moment I had lain awake most of the night contemplating.

My spiralling thoughts were interrupted by a tinkling voice, "So, what's brought you back so quickly? Not that I mind of course. Don't tell me you want a third scone?"

The owner of the cafe stood at the end of the table, her hands resting comfortably on her apron-clad tummy. I remembered she had introduced herself as Mrs A earlier, her surname being the same as the name of the café, but I couldn't now remember it.

"Mrs A, yes, yes. Mrs A... it's Am... erm, Amalti? No, no," I mumbled.

"Amato. It's Café Amato. Are you alright, love? You look like you've seen a ghost."

I returned my notebook to my pocket and fumbled with a packet of sugar, "Maggie always said I was good at keeping things shipshape and didn't know where she would be without me. It's funny I hadn't thought where I would be without her, until it was too late. I'm not good when things don't go as planned, I'm really not." The sugar spilled across the table mat, dissolving into the spilt tea.

Mrs A laid her hand gently on my arm making me jump, "Oh love, you're a bag of nerves! Mr Henderson, isn't it? Sorry, you said you preferred just Henderson."

"You remembered."

"Well, it was only half an hour ago, or so. Your shaking, Henderson, what's happened?"

I nodded, trying to gather the sticky sugar with my sticky fingers. We were of a similar age and her smile was kind, familiar almost, so I felt that perhaps I could confide in her, "Can I ask you a question, Mrs A?"

"Of course," she said, easing herself into the seat opposite and patting a curl of conker-coloured hair back into place. "Fire away."

"Guns... I mean, is gun crime a big problem here?"

She gasped, "Gun crime? In Bexhill? No! What made you ask that?"

"It's... well..." I stumbled. "Just something I heard."

"Guns? I doubt it, this is a peaceful town. My late husband was a policeman here and never once faced a gun." She leaned forward and fixed me with a steely look, "Did you see someone with a gun?"

I paused, remembering Becky's stark warning about keeping silent, then laughed as authentic a chortle as I could muster, "Ha, ha, good grief, no. I overheard someone talking, that's all."

"I see, well, as long as that's all it was. How about another nice warm cheese scone? I think I've got a couple left."

"That would be very kind," I said. "Perhaps two?"

"I'll top your tea up for you, while I'm at it," she rubbed my hand as she rose from the seat. "Oh blast, there's my mobile again. That's three times it's rung in the last five minutes. I'd better see who it is. Two ticks," Mrs A bustled off behind the counter and picked up her phone as it vibrated and repeated a tinny tune beside the till.

I looked out of the café window and found that the continuation of normal life began to soothe me. Old ladies walked reluctant dogs, white-haired men tackled top-heavy ice cream cones, teenaged girls giggled and smoked their way to and from the shops. A giant hairy man spoke urgently into his mobile phone, while a thin man with crooked glasses limped beside him... Carl and Slim!

I shot up from my seat, nearly overturning the table and sending my cup and saucer skimming across the surface. I had to leave, but if I went out the way I came in I would be directly in their path. I looked around and saw Mrs A standing in the door to what I assumed was the kitchen at the rear of the café - there had to be a back door!

Mrs A's smile faded as she saw me dashing towards her and she stepped into my path, "Henderson? Is everything...?"

"I am so sorry, Mrs A, this is rude of me, but I need to leave," I fumbled a few coins from my pocket and pressed them into her hand.

"But your scones? I won't be long, it's just my sister causing a fuss as always," she said, pointing to her phone.

"I'll have them another time, I'm in rather a hurry and need to go out the back. It's a custom where I come from, erm, in the front - out the back."

"I thought you came from Brighton?" she said, as I pushed past her.

"Thank you for the tea," I called, stumbling through the kitchen, out the back door and across the small yard. The gate was stuck, but I managed to yank it open and make my escape down a narrow lane and on to one of Bexhill's busy shopping streets.

I slipped in amongst the oblivious shoppers, scanning the faces for Slim or Carl. I jogged as best I could over the road and headed down a side street, following a sign pointing the way to Bexhill Museum. Another busy place, I calculated, likely to be full of people amongst whom I could disappear and gather my thoughts.

My size isn't really appropriate for running, baked goods being my particular downfall, and I quickly tired. I looked over my shoulder and saw that I was alone, so slowed my pace.

I wasn't due another tablet for hours, but my back pounded with pain. Things had never felt so out of control, even on the day Maggie went and, just as on that awful day, I had no idea what to do.

Overhead a seagull circled and I heard it cry, "Run, run," or that's what my frantic brain thought it said. I wiped my brow with my hanky and set off to take refuge in the museum, just as the loud roar of an engine engulfed me.

Out of a hidden side road came a large, black motorbike with an old-fashioned sidecar attached. It screeched to a halt as the black-helmeted rider turned their head towards me. My heart skipped a beat - they'd sent for reinforcements! Of course they had, that's exactly what they would do.

My wits were spurred into action by another cry from the seagull, who was now sitting on a brown wheelie bin between me and the motorbike. The seagull took angry flight as I grabbed the bin, labelled Garden Waste Only, and threw it down on the ground in front of the bike. There was a muffled cry from inside the rider's helmet, its darkened visor hiding the face of my adversary.

I thumped across the tarmac toward the white building ahead of me, praying it was the museum. I heard the bike roar again and smelled the hot burn of fuel, as the rider reversed and manoeuvred their way around the obstacle. I'd bought myself precious time, but no more than a few seconds.

Bexhill Museum was indeed the long, low building with arched windows along its flank. It had a surprisingly modern entrance of glass and steel, where I heaved open the door much to the surprise of a small white-haired lady standing inside.

"Oh, you gave me a proper start!" she said, clutching the top of her cardigan. "Where did you come from?"

I was panting from my exertions and unable to reply immediately, but stepped into the foyer, trying to get as far from the street as I could.

"Just a moment, I need to do the welcome," the little lady said, as she hopped along beside me. "They make us learn it. Welcome to Bexhill Museum. We have been open since 1914 and have three main galleries, on different floors." Despite my rapid progress further inside, she was managing to keep pace with me, "We also have the Winter Wartime Miniature Railway, dinosaur footprints and all sorts of bones and a collection of historic racing cars. Have you visited us before?"

By this time we had reached a shop area, where another remarkably short lady stood behind a counter, staring at me. Beyond her, a man in an official looking lanyard was speaking urgently into a mobile phone. My mind shot back to Slim, the giant, shouting into his phone a few moments ago... but I was being ridiculous. Not everyone was in cahoots with the gunman, receiving news of a round, cream-suited man who should be apprehended at the earliest opportunity. I took several deep breaths and tried to calm myself.

The lady behind the counter called out to us, "Betty, Betty! We're closing. Did you tell him?"

"Are we?" Betty said. "What time is it, Beryl?"

"Ten to five," Beryl said.

"Is it? Good heavens, I'm having my feet done at a quarter past." Betty turned to me, "I'm ever so sorry, but you'll have to come back another time. We close at five."

"But, but..." I stammered, as I backed against a rack of leaflets, hearing what I thought were muffled engine noises from the street. "I still have ten minutes, don't I? I can have a quick look at everything. The train sounds good, can't I see that?"

Beryl was not to be swayed, however, "No, I can't sell tickets after four forty-five, I'm sorry."

"But..."

"No."

"It's alright, I think we can make an exception for this gentleman." I looked behind Beryl at the man who had come off his phone and was now staring at me with a fixed smile. "You're welcome to stay, sir. Betty, just lock the front door, would you please?"

"Why do you need to lock it?" I asked, my panic rising again.

"For everyone's security," he said.

I turned to Betty, "That doesn't sound right. Shouldn't it be left open when visitors are here?"

"Well, it does seem a little..." she paused and looked at Beryl and then the man in the lanyard.

"It's just to prevent more latecomers, that's all," he said, making his way towards us, his smile fixed like a bayonet, deadly and unyielding.

I began to back away, with Betty tripping along beside me, "There's a three-pound entrance fee and if you have the right change, it would make things a lot easier for Beryl," she chirped.

We had reached the glass entry doors again and I glanced out, "I'm not sure I like being locked in, to be honest."

I couldn't see my dark pursuer or their motorbike, so I decided to take my chances and left the museum without looking back.

"We open at eleven tomorrow," Betty called after me, and I waved over my shoulder as I walked swiftly away.

I had made it barely twenty paces when my shoulders slumped at the heavy throb of the motorbike behind me. Escape had been a silly fantasy. Who was I to outrun a motorbike and a gunman fixed on revenge? Too tired for further pointless flight, I stood still on the pavement. The dark feelings of recent days closed in on me, and I was interested to note that I found an unusual peace in knowing that the decision regarding my fate may well be taken out of my hands.

The motorbike pulled up beside me, "Very well, I am not afraid," I said and, at that moment, I believe I meant it.

The rider reached up and lifted their visor, "You're a hard man to help," Becky said, with some annoyance. "I decided I couldn't just leave you. Get in."

I was stunned.

"Come on, we don't have all day," and she handed me a second helmet, which had been hooked over her arm. She then gestured to the sidecar, "Get in!"

"In there?" I asked.

"Yes, you'll fit."

I tried not to be offended, as that had not been my primary concern, "But won't people see us? Them, the bad people?"

She shrugged, "If they do, they won't catch us. I know my way around town and can go places on this they wouldn't even dream of. Come on, we need to talk."

I decided to place myself in her apparently capable hands, largely because we really did need to talk – about far more than she knew. I worked my way into the sidecar and as I put on my helmet, Becky asked, "What's your name?"

"Howard," I replied, wincing as pain shot in a circle around my hips, which were stuffed like oversized sardines in an undersized can. "Howard Henderson, but everyone calls me Henderson."

"Okay, Henderson, are you ready for an adventure?" she said with a grin, as she revved the engine to an extraordinary pitch.

"Actually, I think I may have had more adventure today than I can really cope with," but my words were lost to her as we tore off at enormous and, in my humble opinion, quite unnecessary speed.

# CHAPTER 3

Racing along, my rear skimming a fraction above the surface of the road, would have been a great adventure for many – but not for me. With the wind whipping my face and every joint being shaken apart, I was reminded that more than a hundred years ago Bexhill was the location of the first British motor race, and I imagined the conditions then were not dissimilar to those I was currently enduring.

As the bike started to slow and Becky brought us to a merciful halt, I opened an eye to see a short run of wooden beach huts at our side. She informed me that we were away from the main town in an area called Cooden, which seemed to offer little more than sand dunes and miles of stony shoreline heading west towards Pevensey Bay.

She left me to unfold myself from the sidecar, for which I was grateful. Away from the judgement of observers, I heaved myself out and gingerly realigned my joints. I then hobbled onto the beach and around the end of the row of half a dozen fat little huts that sat facing the sea. The double front doors were open on the nearest one, and I stood for a moment to admire the structure. It was entirely made of wood, painted some time ago in what must have once been a jaunty canary yellow. It had a pitched roof overhanging the front to provide cover for a small terrace which had a low balustrade picked out in white. A driftwood sign, worn smooth by the waves, declared it - *The Lazy Dayz Beach Hut*. I couldn't help but wince at the inappropriate second *Z*, but let it pass as Becky brought out two long seat cushions.

"Strawberry Thief!"

Becky turned sharply, "What?"

"The fabric - William Morris's classic design of The Strawberry Thief. Upholstery is my trade."

"Oh, right, well done," she said, placing them on benches either side of the terrace and going back inside.

"Morris based the pattern on the birds that stole the strawberries from his kitchen garden."

Becky returned with a bottle of beer in her hand and declared, "Aren't you a mine of useless information. Beer?"

"Oh, erm, no, thank you. Do you have tea?"

"There's a kettle inside," she waved vaguely towards the interior with her bottle, then lay back on a bench closing her eyes.

This gave me the opportunity to examine her properly, this overall-clad woman, my daughter, who I was unaware even existed until yesterday. I knew that she was thirty-three years of age, but beyond that, her long legs, pale almond skin and thick eyelashes were all new to me. She had at least five silver earrings in each ear and her hair was cut short, in an edgy, choppy style. The roots were black and yet the remainder of her hair had been dyed a mixture of silver and grey, giving it the look of burnished steel. It was impressive, if a little unorthodox.

She suddenly opened an eye, "I'll have to charge you if you stand there looking at me much longer."

Heat rushed to my cheeks, "Oh, yes, of course, sorry. I was... well... how did you know I hadn't... you know?"

"Moved?" She closed her eyes again, "You're standing on the beach. I didn't hear you crunching over the pebbles. Doesn't take a genius."

"No, no, of course not," I quickly crunched my way off the beach and into The Lazy Dayz Beach Hut.

It was surprisingly neat and clean. I breathed deeply, the orderliness calming me after this afternoon's unexpected activity. Multiple shelves held crockery and glasses, alongside carefully labelled tins of tea and coffee. It was really quite homely, even more so when I had the kettle hissing on the little gas stove. I was impressed by Becky's housekeeping – perhaps that was something she had acquired from my DNA, as I could see nothing of my short legs, heavy frame or red hair about her.

Five minutes later, I was sitting opposite her with a large mug of milky tea, watching the sun make its lazy way toward the horizon.

It was some time before she spoke, "Look, Henderson, whatever you heard back there, I'm not a thief. I don't steal from people... not really." She sniffed and took a sip of her beer. I wondered if I had been more present in her life, would she now be using a glass?

"I see," I said. "Actually, I don't see at all. Clearly that chap, Carl, is not a nice person, but you do have something of his. Can I ask what it is?"

"No, you can't."

"I see." I waited, but she appeared to have nothing more to say on the matter. In the awkward silence I noticed that my feet were throbbing from all the charging about – I really wasn't used to moving at such speed. "My feet are a little swollen," I said. "Would it offend you if I removed my shoes?"

"Doesn't bother me."

I began to undo my laces, "My days of leather soled shoes are over, but even with these softer ones I'm a martyr to my feet, I'm afraid. Maggie wouldn't allow talk of anything but handmade brogues – for us both."

"Who's Maggie?" Becky asked.

"She was my wife. She died," I said, the words still raw even a year later.

"Oh, sorry. What happened?"

I felt the familiar black dog creeping closer again, "A heart attack. It was very sudden. Instant really."

"Sorry. It must be crap not being able to say goodbye, but at least it was quick. My mum took eight months to die. Shitty cancer," she said, shifting on her cushion.

"I know, I'm very sorry."

"How do you know?" Becky sat up and swung round, "You knew Mum?"

"Yes, that's why I came to your garage. It was a long time ago and we lost contact when we were young."

"How did you know she'd died then?"

"I got a letter from her."

"No, you can't have done, I mean, she died seventeen years ago."

"So, I understand. It was sent care of my mother in Rye, where we grew up."

Her eyes widened, "Yes, she went to school there."

"Hazel and I were best friends as children. We did everything together. She encouraged me to misbehave - which didn't come naturally, and I encouraged her to conform - which was equally alien to her. We were quite a team."

"But how could she write to you? I was fifteen when she died. It's not possible." She looked at me with an understandable amount of scepticism, "What are you trying to pull?"

"Nothing, I assure you, Becky," I said, hastily producing the letter from my jacket pocket, embarrassed to find that it was moist from my exertions. "This is her letter. Please, let me explain. She vanished when we were eighteen, without a word. I couldn't find her, no-one could. I had no idea why she'd gone; I just couldn't understand it. I now realise that she had found herself pregnant – had I known, I would have done the right thing, I assure you…"

"Wait, are you saying…? Are you my father?"

I tried not to hear disappointment in her voice, but I couldn't help but think it was there, "Yes, I am, according to your mother."

A flash of anger crossed her face, "You think she lied?"

"No, no, not at all. It's in her letter," I said, holding it out. "May I read it to you? You are welcome to read it… but it may need a little time to dry."

She moved away from it, "I don't want to touch it."

"Yes, probably wise."

"I mean, is it really from her, from Mum?"

I took the letter from its envelope and held it out to her. It moved limply in the breeze as she bent forward and studied it from a little way away.

"It does look like her writing. But I don't get it. You're my dad? Why didn't she tell me? Anyway, how could it have taken all this time to get to you?"

"I know, it's a lot to take in. She explains it all in the letter. May I read it? Her words are far better than me trying to explain it."

"Her words? After seventeen years," Becky stood and turned towards the sea. "That's... I mean... go on then, read it," she said in a small voice.

"*Dear Henderson,*" I read. "It's funny, it reminded me that Hazel was the one who first started using my surname, when I told her I didn't like the name Howard."

Becky shrugged, "Fascinating. What does she say?"

"Yes, sorry. She goes on, *When you receive this letter, I will have been dead a long time.* I know this sounds like something from a crime novel, and I read a lot of them, but..."

She spun round her eyes red and angry, "Please, for God's sake, just tell me what the hell is going on? Why is my mother, who I buried years ago, sending letters to some random bloke who claims to be my father?"

I have to say, I thought this was a very fair question.

"Your mother knew she was dying when she wrote this letter. She gave it to a solicitor, a chap called Mr Moon."

Becky nodded, "Yes, I remember him, he dealt with her estate."

"It's his son now, Simon Moon, who by sheer coincidence is also my solicitor, and has been helping me put my affairs in order."

"He never said anything to me about a letter, when he went through the will and everything."

"No, Hazel had been very clear that the letter was only to be posted to me when you reached the age of thirty-three, the age she was when she died." I referred to the letter which was slowly crisping-up as the sea breeze dried it, "She says, *I only felt that I understood the world and my place in it during this last year of my life. I hope that when Becky reaches this age, she may want to know more about who she is.*"

"So, you didn't know you had a daughter?" she asked, as she sat back on the bench opposite me.

"No, not until this arrived yesterday. We were young and Hazel says she didn't want to burden me with a child.  On the night in question, she had persuaded me to try some lethal tequila shots. We were pretty innocent, as hard as that may be to believe as we quaffed tequila, but we were. Somehow in our drunken state we agreed to practice kissing on each other, then one thing led to another and our clumsy experimentation became... well, more than kissing. I imagine you get the picture; hearing of your parent's intimate life is not comfortable for any child."

"I am not a child and you are not my parent!" she

31

jumped up and stepped out on to the beach.

"No, of course, I quite understand," I said, following her to the edge of the terrace. "What I meant was, it appears our experimentation led to you. She was very clear in her letter that she doesn't regret our actions. She says she had the most incredible life with you. I wish I'd been able to see her before the end. Hazel was a good friend to me." I paused as I thought back to the speech I should have given in the garage hours ago, "Becky, she wanted me to find you and introduce myself. I'm here to do that, but I do not intend to disturb your life or attempt to assume any role within it. That would not be possible... not in the long term. Of course, meeting you is very... nice, too."

"Nice?"

"Yes, well, more than nice, of course, but it's odd, isn't it?"

I watched Becky as she slowly wrapped her arms around herself. The waves filled the silence with a gentle soundtrack and we stood quietly, as if in respect to Hazel and her absence from both our lives.

Becky took a deep breath, "You're not what I expected."

"No, I don't imagine I am."

"But at least you came. I was convinced my father was a shit of the highest order. Mum would never talk about him, so I assumed he'd just dumped her or something. But if you didn't know about me until yesterday, then maybe it's not your fault."

"Thank you. Did Hazel... your mother, ever marry?"

"Nope. It was just her and me."

"I see." I sipped my tea while she wiped her cheek with

the back of her hand.

"What am I supposed to say to you? Should we hug or something?"

I stiffened, "Do you want to hug?"

"Not really."

"Good, I mean, that's fine. Perhaps we should talk about the here and now - the events of this afternoon?"

She started towards the sea, "Let's walk."

I hastily put down my mug and reached for my shoes.

"Don't bother with them, there's sand at the edge of the waves," she said, as she sat on a ridge of pebbles to undo her hefty mechanic's boots.

I shivered as I looked across the stony stretch between me and the sea. Beaches and I were not natural companions, and the idea of walking across stones, shells and all manner of dog detritus filled me with horror. However, I still had some catching up to do in terms of first impressions, so I bit my tongue and set off towards her.

The pain was excruciating as every rock stabbed my doughy flesh, but I ploughed on, choosing to talk rather than chance crying out, "So, what sort of... work... do you... *ouch*... do... in the... *ouch*... garage? Appointments and... so on?"

"I'm the mechanic," she said, as she removed her socks and placed them in her boots.

"Oh... ouch... excellent," I said, masking the pain of my final few steps as I lunged for the soft, wet sand ahead of me. "Do you own the business?"

"No, a friend does. I rang him this afternoon and he went in and checked Carl had gone, then locked up the doors they'd damaged," she stood and began to walk west, along the shore.

"You knew he wasn't dead?" I asked, as I came alongside her, the cold sand and lapping waves soothing my throbbing feet.

"Not straight away, but while I was grabbing my stuff I heard him groan. I checked and he hadn't got any bullet holes in him, so I think he just brained himself on the car when he fell over with shock, stupid sod. Look, this has nothing to do with you, Henderson. Nice to meet you, put a face to the name and all that, but I don't need a dad. I've managed without one up 'til now, so go home. At the moment they have no idea who you are, it'll all blow over when they realise there's been no come back on them."

I was supremely tempted to head straight for the station, my task here was complete according to Hazel's letter, but there was an itch at the back of my skull Maggie had always called the Henderson Niggle. Something was not right.

"I am aware that my assistance may be limited, but I can't go home without knowing if you are in any more danger. I owe that to your mother, as well as to you."

She looked at me and I noticed her grey eyes were an almost perfect match for her hair and really rather pretty, "You're assuming I don't have anyone else to look after me, like a boyfriend."

"Ah, yes, good point. Do you?"

"No."

"What's going on Becky? I know his name is Carl, the big chap is Slim – which seems rather unfair, but there we are – and Carl was calling for someone by the name of Ellis. Who are these people?"

She stopped, "Ellis? Are you sure he said Ellis?"

"Yes, he said it twice, *call Ellis, call Ellis* – I'm sure of it."

She pulled a mobile phone from the breast pocket of her blue overall and began to type, "Interesting. Maybe Ellis is Seven..."

"Ellis is seven? He's a bit young to be involved with all this, isn't he?"

"I think I need to take you to meet the others before you go, just in case there's anything else you can tell us, come on," she said and hurried back to her boots, skipping with admirable agility up the beach to the hut.

I hurried behind her and prepared to face the tortuous return across the rocky terrain. However, by the time I was level with the hut and ready for the second crossing, Becky was standing before me with my shoes in her hand.

"Here, I don't think we need to re-enact Riverdance across the stones again, do we?"

I think I may have blushed, but my relief was enormous, "No, perhaps not." I sat down gingerly and began to brush the sand from my socks... No, no, no! I had been walking in the sea in my socks! I covered them with my hands and glanced up at Becky.

"Wet socks?" she asked, with what can only be described as a smirk, but it was not, perhaps, an unkind one.

"Why didn't you tell me?"

She shrugged, "How was I to know you didn't like paddling in your socks, or have deformed feet you don't like to show people or..."

"Yes, well... this sort of thing is not my normal territory," I said, my embarrassment now complete. "I don't think I've ever done anything reckless enough to warrant becoming a hunted man. I'm not thinking straight."

Then, as if by magic, a reminder of another pursuer burst from my jacket pocket with the opening bars of Wagner's The Ride of the Valkyries.

# CHAPTER 4

I struggled to retrieve the phone, my fingers swollen to sausage proportions by the heat of the day, "Will she never leave me alone?"

"I heard that tune earlier, just before you shot at Carl," Becky said.

"Hm, you would have done. Maggie set individual ring tones for specific people. She thought it was funny - this one's for my mother. If I had known how to change it back, I would have... actually, that's not true, I would never change anything she did," I fell silent as I pictured Maggie at her desk smiling and waving her paint-stained fingers at me.

Becky sat down beside me, "I think your mother is saying something," she said, pointing to the phone in my hand.

I looked down, "Oh, yes, of course." I lifted it to my ear, "Mother, I'm here... Yes, I know you rang earlier... Yes, I am with her now... No, you can't speak to her... because it's not appropriate. I have to go. I'll ring you later when I'm back at the guest house. I really have to go, my socks are wet," and I ended the call. "Wet socks will give her something to worry about until later."

"My granny," Becky said, pulling a face. "It seems funny to have sprouted a grandmother at my age."

"It must do, but you may choose not to engage with this one when you meet her... if you want to, that is."

She got to her feet and headed back to the hut, "I'll think about it."

As I put my shoes on, I did think that my mother's life-long advice about the dangers of wet socks might not be misjudged. Trench foot was not what I needed at the moment amongst everything else.

I staggered back across the beach to find Becky waiting for me with a blanket and pillow, "I have to go into town for a while to set up a meeting with the others," she said.

"What others?"

She shrugged, "I'll tell you later, there are seven of us... it's a bit complicated, but I'm not alone in this. I won't be long, but I thought you might fancy a snooze or something. You look like you could do with it. These bench cushions fit on the beds inside so you can lie down out of the sun. You've gone a bit pink."

I put my hand to my high forehead and could feel the heat from the sun pulsing there, "Thank you, I wouldn't normally expose myself for so long at this time of year. You're lucky not to have inherited my pale skin, I suppose you take after your mother. Although, if I remember, her skin was..."

She thrust the pillow at me, "Do you want this or not? I need to go." Throwing the blanket onto the outside bench she walked away, her crash helmet over her arm. A few moments later the sound of the bike rumbled through the air and she was gone.

Had I said something to offend her, or did she actually need to leave to make arrangements for this unexplained meeting? Whatever her reason, the thought of a catnap was now overwhelming. She must think I'm safe here, I told myself, as I moved the cushion inside and settled down on a long wooden bench. It was rock hard and I was positive I stood little chance of sleep coming, but my body felt otherwise and I was soon fast asleep.

As I woke, I had a vague recollection of torrid dreams. I had been running along beaches, chased by tiny gunmen in cardigans, gun fire all around me, bells ringing, seagulls rising out of wheelie bins... but it was time for another tablet and I tried to put it from my mind. Task completed, I moved out onto the terrace grumbling at my body's inability to deal with its disintegration with more grace, and noticed my phone lying on the floor.

I must have dropped it in my haste to rest, and it appeared I had missed several calls from an unknown number, but a message had been left for me;

*"Mr Henderson? Mr Henderson, it's Mary, from the Sunnyside Guest House,"* she was whispering so quietly I could only just hear her. *"I'm so sorry to disturb you, but I'm really not sure I've done the right thing. They said they were your brothers, but there is an awful lot of banging and crashing coming from your room. The larger gentleman was not at all pleasant, not like you. Although your other brother, the slim one, is quite the opposite, rather charming. But it doesn't seem right. I hope that... Oh, now stop..."*

I stared at the phone as her voice was replaced by a collection of pops and crackles, before a final, distant cry that sounded a lot like "... *jam cupboard!*" preceded the abrupt end of the message.

I have never yodelled, but I managed a strangled version of one when Becky appeared without warning around the side of the hut at just that moment.

"For goodness sake, Becky! You frightened the life out of me."

"Didn't you hear the bike?"

"No! I was focused on the unfolding chaos caused by my actions earlier today. I need to call the police."

She snatched the phone firmly from my grasp, "No, you can't."

"You don't understand, there's a woman in danger."

"Listen, I don't know what you dreamed or imagined, but you're safe here."

"Becky, I got a voicemail from the landlady of the guest house I'm staying in. Two men claiming to be my brothers, who do not exist by the way – one large, who I assume is Slim and, one slim, who I assume is Carl – gosh, that's confusing. The point is, Carl and Slim are currently, or recently, ransacking my room and may well have attacked Mary, the landlady."

As I drew breath, Becky took a step back frowning, "How did she...? I mean, are you sure?"

"Absolutely, listen," I said and proceeded to play her the message. "You see, we need to get the police round to the Sunnyside Guest House as soon as possible."

Becky began pacing to and fro on the small terrace, "No, we can't, it'll be fatal for me and the others. No police."

"I don't understand, we can't leave Mary in distress and they could be doing anything with my belongings. We have to do something."

"Alright, alright, maybe we can swing past on our way into town, just to check she's okay."

I am not sure where my sudden bravado came from, but it had arrived in the nick of time, "We will do more than drive by, Becky. We must go in and face these people and help Mary. At once!"

I felt a sense of purpose that had been absent for far too long and an unexpected ripple of excitement passed through me. I put my phone firmly in my pocket and set off at a quick march toward the infernal motorbike.

"Henderson!" Becky said, holding her hand out to stop me.

"I will not be put off," I said, until I stepped from the hut's terrace and plunged my bare feet into an agonising mass of pebbles. "Ow, ow, ouch!" I hopped quickly back on to the smooth wooden boards and limped inside to retrieve the shoes and soggy socks that I had removed before going to sleep.

As I sat and put them on, the frustration of my physical inadequacies rendered me silent. Becky was sensitive enough to say nothing as she changed out of her overalls, to reveal denim jeans and a lilac and blue checked shirt. She picked up a short leather jacket and locked up the beach hut behind me as I made my way to the bike.

"Are you sure about this?" she called. "It could get pretty nasty if they're still there, we don't know what they might do to you... or me."

I began to squeeze myself into the sidecar, "My safety is no longer important, I'll go in alone. I can't risk anyone getting hurt by my own stupidity. Please, can we go." We needed to move swiftly, as I was concerned that I was talking the talk of confrontation, but had limited confidence in my ability to follow it through.

✵ ✵ ✵

It didn't take us long to get to South Cliff, the wide road containing large detached villas, gaudy mansions and the guest house. Becky parked us in a neighbouring road, hopped off and came round to pull me out of the sidecar, "You should really take better care of yourself, what are you, fifty-five? Sixty?"

"I am fifty," I wheezed.

"Blimey, well, even more reason to get yourself loosened up a bit."

"It's been a long day."

"Fair enough," she said and took my helmet, attaching it with hers to the frame of the motorbike.

"Do you own a car, by any chance?"

"Nope, this is my baby. I put her back together with my own hands. It took three years and she is never going anywhere without me."

"Excellent. What an achievement!" I said, hoping that I sounded sincere.

We began to walk down the road to the corner of South Cliff, "I thought you said these people wouldn't know who

I was? If so, how do you think they found out where I was staying?"

"No idea. They're well connected in the town, I suppose."

We approached Sunnyside cautiously, keeping close to the hedges and walls of the neighbouring properties, "The big gate's shut at the front, is that normal?" Becky asked.

"Mary told me that after 5pm it's closed and guests need to ring the bell."

"Damn, that's going to be tricky."

"Not really," I said, as I raised my hand to press the buzzer on the intercom. "I just need to..."

"Stop," she hissed. "What are you doing?"

"Asking Mary to open the gate," I said, a little surprised at her tone.

"Not that way, jeez! We need to get in without attracting attention. We don't want Carl answering the door and shooting us, do we?"

"Shooting us? Do you think he has another gun?"

"I have no idea, but we know he has one gun, don't we?"

"Becky, are you telling me that you gave him back his gun?"

"I didn't exactly give it back to him," she said. "When I thought you'd killed him, I cleaned your fingerprints off it and laid it beside him. I had no idea he was going to rise from the dead. When he did, I just legged it."

"I really don't want to offer any criticism so early on in our relationship, Becky, but do you really think leaving a loaded gun lying around for anyone to pick up was a good idea?"

"At that point, *Daddy-dearest,* there was one hell of a lot to think about, because you behaved like a dick and thought firing the gun was a good idea."

I understood her point, "I apologise, I may have been blunt and you're right, we are both to blame."

"That's not what I said... never mind," she said, through gritted teeth. "Is there a back-way into this place?"

"Not that I'm aware of. My room is at the back and the garden seemed to have a pretty solid wall around it and another property directly behind."

She looked around to check we were not being watched, "Right then, you'll have to go over the wall."

I examined the brick wall that towered above our heads, "Wouldn't it be simpler to call the police and let them deal with it? I mean, I didn't kill him after all and committed no real crime, yet they're breaking and entering."

Becky sighed, "Henderson, you don't get it, do you? I'm in this up to my neck and we are not going to the police. Now, let's do this. At least it's garden bin day and we know you're pretty handy with them from earlier," she nipped across the neatly cut grass verge and pulled a wheelie bin from the curb back to the wall. She patted the lid, "Up you pop, I can give you a push from behind if need be."

"I'm not entirely sure..."

"You said you wanted to help, so this is your chance, Daddy-dearest," she said, with a grin.

"No, no, after you, *Daughter-dearest,*" I said, with a deep bow.

"Get on the damn thing," Becky growled, and I gathered our exchange of banter was over.

I clung onto the lid and hopped a couple of times to gain the momentum needed to lift me up. Becky stood back and watched with what I hoped was growing admiration. As I grappled my way onto the bin, I heard Maggie's, telling me to, *suck in that belly and get a move on.* The brown bin wobbled unnervingly under my weight, but I held my balance and was able to haul myself up, with a fair amount of shoving from Becky, to sit astride the top of the wall.

As the thrill of my physical achievement settled over me, I blew out my cheeks with pride, "Phew! Excellent, that wasn't so bad. Your turn."

"No way, I can't stand heights."

I looked down at her, almost toppling back onto the pavement, "What? Why didn't you tell me that before I got up here?"

"Because one of us had to go up and see if we could open the gate from the inside, and I knew it couldn't be me."

"So, what was your plan for me to get down the other side?" I said, looking at the drop that ended in a bed of pink-flowering hydrangea bushes far below me. "Do you really think..." I didn't get to finish my sentence, as Becky reached up from below, grabbed my dangling foot and shoved with all her might. My grip on the wall was tenuous at best and this was enough to send me flying over and down into the garden below.

After a minute or two in the hydrangea's embrace, gathering my thoughts and what was left of my dignity, I rolled out to find her sitting crossed-legged on the grass tapping happily on her phone.

"Well, that's another accomplishment to add to my curriculum vitae," I said, removing a twig from my collar.

Becky giggled and slipped her phone away before flicking pink petals from the top of my head, "I didn't know you could be funny."

I couldn't help but smile.

"Wait a minute, how did you get in here?"

"There's a smaller door set inside the big gate, I just tried it and it opened. Bit lax on security here, aren't they?" She grinned, then looked back at the house, "It seems quiet, but we need to go in carefully. Come on."

Perhaps instinctively, Becky held out her hand and I took it as she guided me quietly across the grass. It was a simple but extraordinary moment. Human contact can mean so many things, but this first touch between father and child was intoxicating. I began to understand the appeal of parenthood, something that Maggie and I had deliberately sidestepped.

Becky pushed open the large oak front door and we stood hand in hand listening for signs of life. There was nothing. As we entered the hall Becky released my hand, the loss of her touch startling for a second, so natural had it felt.

She turned to the right and peered into the breakfast room, which was empty., I was standing beside an excellent rosewood chiffonier of the Regency period, with a mirror attached to the top, "Becky," I called in a whisper and she crept back to me.

"What?"

"Look at this," I pointed to the wall beside the mirror, where a darker patch of paint was visible. "The light has faded the paint on the wall, but not in this area."

"So, what?"

"The chiffonier has recently been moved to the right. Doesn't that seem odd to you?" I gestured to a small door hidden in the oak panelling that covered part of the hall, "It's now covering that door."

Becky put her ear against the panel, "I can hear something. Does Mary have a dog?"

"No, she told me there were no pets allowed, due to her allergies."

"In which case, there's someone in here."

We looked at each other, "It must be Mary," I said.

"Help me shift it."

We slowly slid the tall chest along the polished floor. Once it was clear of the door, I knocked gently, "Mary?" I whispered. "It's Henderson. Is that you?"

For a moment there was nothing, then the door silently swung open and the doll-like face of Mary, the owner of Sunnyside Guest House, peered out, her eyes wide and lips trembling.

"Mr Henderson? Oh, thank goodness. They put me in the cupboard, Mr Henderson. My jam cupboard!"

"I'm so sorry, Mary. We need to know where they are, the men who said they were my brothers?"

We all froze as a floorboard creaked above our heads. Mary pointed up at the ceiling, "They're upstairs."

# CHAPTER 5

The noise from the floor above stopped and the Sunnyside returned to silence. Becky put her finger to her lips and looked fiercely at us both, Mary and I nodded mutely in understanding. I assumed we were about to run and with my recent successful ascent of the wall, not to mention elderly Mary in the line-up, I hoped I might not be the worst on the starting blocks for a change.

However, instead of heading outside, Becky pointed to the cupboard and began moving Mary back through the small door. At first, she resisted, but was no match for Becky who soon had her tucked away inside. Then she turned to me and indicated that I was next, but I shook my head and pointed to the chiffonier. I then pantomimed the fact that it was not wise to leave it in the middle of the hall revealing that it had been moved. After several attempts, increasingly fierce arm waving and the risk of a rotator cuff injury, I got my point across.

Becky cursed quietly, but I stood my ground. Details mattered to me and meant I was an excellent problem-solver. Admittedly, the problems were usually limited to calculating fabric requirements to pattern-match a complex armchair cover, or try to come up with the guilty party before the detective in a novel, but nevertheless it was something I was good at.

Another creak from the floor above sent us both toward the cupboard, and we hovered in the doorway. Everything went quiet again. I looked at the large piece of furniture, then at the rug below our feet. At a quick glance, I could tell that it was Persian and probably merino wool with silk details, but most importantly it was large enough to sit under the chiffonier.

I pointed at the chest, then down to the rug, mimed putting one on top of the other and then sliding it along the floor. After my third attempt, Becky hissed at me, "Alright, Quasimodo, give it a rest."

"We need to move the chiffonier onto the rug," I mouthed in return.

"The what?"

"The chiffonier – the chest of drawers, then we can slide it into place easily from inside the cupboard."

"Brilliant," she said, which I thought was nice of her.

We retrieved Mary from the cupboard, then silently lifted the chiffonier onto the rug; me and her on one side and Becky on the other. Then we bundled Mary back into the cupboard and slid the rug and its load as close to the position we had found it in as we could. We left enough room for us both to slip into the cupboard behind it, then Becky was able to reach around the partially closed door, grab the edge of the rug and slide the whole thing back into place.

The cupboard was small, dark and stuffy. There was a fine line of light that ran down between the door and its frame, allowing me to make out narrow shelves surrounding us, on which I could see copious jars of jams and preserves.

"I made those myself, from the apple and plum trees in the garden," Mary whispered.

"Sshh, quiet," Becky hissed.

"Sorry," Mary said.

We waited, but there was no further sound from the house - Carl and Slim appeared to be none the wiser regarding our presence below them.

"They've been up there ever such a long time," Mary said, through trembling lips.

"If they overheard you leaving me that warning message, I bet they decided to lay in wait, assuming I would come back."

I could just make out Becky's pale head nodding, "They must want to find out if you told anyone about them. Interrogate you," she said.

I felt a little queasy and wondered if it would be feasible to make a break for the toilet.

"How long do you think we will have to wait?" Mary whispered.

"They could be here for hours," I said, my bladder throbbing at the thought of being in this cupboard all night.

"Nah, they'll be on the move soon," Becky said, and we were suddenly illuminated by the screen of her mobile phone coming to life. "I'm going to text Seven and arrange a meet in fifteen minutes to give back what I took from them."

"Seven? That's an unusual name," Mary said. "Mind you, children are called all sorts these days."

Becky grinned, "We think he's called Ellis. Seven is just what we call him, as there are seven of us in the circle. He's Carl and Slim's boss."

"I don't really understand..."

"It's complicated, Mary," I said, not wanting to let on that I had little idea what Becky was talking about either.

"I'm going to tell him to meet me at the seafront colonnade," Becky continued. "Hopefully, if Seven sees the message straight away, it should only take a couple of minutes for him to alert those two upstairs, five minutes for them to leave and get to the seafront, twenty minutes to wait for me and realise I'm not coming, then another five minutes to get back here. That'll give us plenty of time to grab your stuff and disappear."

"Why can't we call the police?" Mary asked, not unreasonably. "They took my phone when they put me in here, or I would have done it myself."

"Erm, we can't," Becky mumbled, finishing her text.

"It's complicated, Mary," I repeated. After a moment's hesitation, I felt an unusual surge of confidence and started to talk with no idea where I was heading, "You see, erm, Mary, this is part of a wider operation and we are not quite ready to arrest them yet. We need to bide our time before taking action."

I could make out Mary's heart-shaped face turn to mine in the gloom and her eyes were wide, "Mr Henderson, are you an undercover spy?"

Becky snorted, but I squared my shoulders and ignored her, "Something like that, Mary. So, you can see the importance of not revealing what's happened, can't you?"

"Oh, yes, absolutely. How exciting! I would never have known it of you Mr Henderson, to look at you."

Becky snorted again, "He's a master of disguise. He even has a code name."

"Really? Oh, Mr Henderson, you are marvellous. What is it? Can you tell me?"

I glared at Becky, who was clearly enjoying herself a little too much, "Well, erm, it's not something I can really..."

"Oh, go on, tell her. Mary looks like someone we can trust," she sniggered.

Mary nodded eagerly, her eyes full of awe and admiration, "I won't tell a soul. What's your codename?"

I know that Becky was teasing, but looking into Mary's eyes made me feel bold, "The Seagull," I said.

Why I chose The Seagull, I will never know, but it had a significant effect on both my cupboard companions. Becky turned away with a strange wheezing noise and buried her head amongst the jars of jam. Mary nodded her head slowly and repeated the name with hushed reverence, "The Seagull. Oh, Mr Henderson..."

Luckily, we were interrupted by the sound of feet coming down the stairs, one light tread and a second slower and heavier. They must have received the message about the meeting and the footsteps headed towards the front door.

"What about her in the cupboard?" a voice said,

sounding a lot like Slim.

"Leave her. They'll probably send us back when we've got the stuff off Becky."

"Fair do's," Slim said and we heard them exit the house.

"Let's wait a few minutes, make sure they've gone," Becky said.

We stood in the darkness, with just the sound of our breathing to occupy us. Soon we could hear what I imagined was an electric mechanism opening the front gate.

"There's a sensor that opens it from the inside if there's a car on the drive," Mary said. "That big fellow probably set it off. It wouldn't have known he wasn't a car."

"Right, let's get out of here. Come on, Seagull," Becky said and she pushed against the door. I tried my best to ignore her chuckles and helped as best I could. Between us we created enough momentum to slide the rug and its chiffonier cargo away.

Once we were in the hall, Becky checked her watch, "We need to be gone in about twenty minutes. Henderson, do you want to go and grab your things? In case they come back."

"Yes, of course," I said. "I'll take the opportunity to freshen up and change my clothes, as well."

"No, absolutely not. We've only got twenty minutes."

"I am aware of the timeline, Becky, but... well... I have never been on the run before, but I imagine I will be much better at coping with it if I am in fresh underwear and clean trousers," and I almost bounded up the twisting oak staircase before she could object.

The door to my room was standing open and I gingerly stepped inside. I gasped as I saw the mess they had left behind. My clothes had been strewn across the bed and floor, my bag was turned inside out and thrown in a corner, every drawer and cupboard were open. I quickly gathered it all together and, after years of packing for both Maggie and I, had everything rolled and packed into my travel bag in a jiffy. After five more minutes I felt revived, having washed my face and cleaned my teeth. After another five, I was dressed in fresh undies, a clean peacock-blue silk shirt, navy-blue corduroys and was ready to go back downstairs. My remaining hair takes little maintenance, so I gave it one last check in the mirror and smoothed it to one side with the palm of my hand. I paused to look at my face, which had worn a rather grey pallor in recent weeks, but now seemed to have regained some if its colour – not just from too much south coast sunshine either. Perhaps a little adventure was proving to be good for me.

Becky was pacing back and forth as I came down the stairs, "Blimey, that was quick."

I smiled at her, approached the small reception desk and rang the bell.

"Now what are you doing?" Becky said, standing by the front door.

"I need to check out."

"Really?"

"Yes, really... ah, Mary, may I please check out?" I said, as she bustled out of the kitchen.

"I am so sorry for letting those men in, Mr Henderson. I hope it hasn't ruined your visit to Bexhill. You will come back, won't you."

"I'm not sure that will be possible, but thank you. Now, what do I owe you?"

Mary would only let me pay for the one night I had actually slept at the Sunnyside and I wished her a pleasant evening. She pressed a button which allowed the gate to open at the end of the drive. She closed the gate behind us and we heard her bolting the smaller door from the inside, so Carl and Slim couldn't get back in should they return later.

As we made our way back down the street, Becky asked, "Did they take anything?"

"Oh, I didn't think to check," I replied, putting my bag on the pavement and unzipping it.

"Not now," Becky said, grabbing the bag. "We need to go before they come back."

South Cliff was clear and there was no sign of Carl or Slim, so we hurried round the corner and reclaimed the motorbike. As I squeezed myself into the sidecar, she placed my bag on my lap and pulled out her phone, "Brill, Seven is fuming about me not turning up," she said and began to type a reply.

"What are you saying? You really don't want to stir a hornet's nest and make it worse."

"No, I've said I'm trying to find you, so I'm delayed," she put the phone back in her pocket. "I told him he'd get his money back soon."

"So, it was money you took from them."

"Yes, it was."

"Was it a lot?" I asked.

"Not really, I thought it was small enough not to be missed – but apparently not."

"Indeed."

She mounted the motorbike and settled onto her seat, "What's that on your bag?"

I looked down, "A luggage label. Why?"

"What does it say on it?"

"My details, in case of loss or theft."

"Hell!" she exclaimed loudly. "Has it got your name and address on it?"

"Yes, of course."

"Double hell! Don't you see? They can track you down now they've seen that. There's no way you can go home or they'll come and find you."

"Yes, of course. Do you really think they'd go to Brighton, to my home?"

"Possibly, where are your house keys?"

"In my pocket, attached to a tag sewn in for security purposes."

"At least they haven't got them. Do you have home security or an alarm or something?"

I began to feel sweat breaking out again and panic rising up towards me, "No, it's a maisonette above my upholstery business. I really can't let them break in, not now, with everything..."

"You don't have an alarm? No CCTV?"

"No, nothing."

"And I suppose you leave a key under a plant pot outside the door?" she asked, with undisguised sarcasm.

"I am not that foolish, Becky. It's behind a loose brick at the bottom of the door frame."

"For crying out loud!"

I started to remove my helmet, "This is a disaster."

"Look, Henderson, it's probably okay. They're only looking for *you*, they probably won't be interested in your house."

"Becky, you don't understand. They cannot get into my flat, they can't, not this week. Everything is on my desk. Labelled, laminated, easy to access – my whole life. I have to go back." Not only had I sorted out matters with my solicitor, I had also begun to put in order all my domestic paperwork at home. It was laid out across my desk; folders relating to my funeral, bank accounts, investments and so on. In my distress I began climb out of the sidecar, but she pushed me back down.

I clung to my travel bag, every cancerous cell in my body seemed to be screaming with torture as I began to overheat. How had it come to this? How had I become some sort of fugitive, on the run, within the space of a few hours? Until now, I had been an almost invisible citizen, not even a parking ticket in fifty years.

I had planned this week so meticulously; I had it all written in my little notebook, which I felt for in my trouser pocket. As my fingers gripped it tightly through the corduroy fabric, I could picture the schedule it contained. At this moment I should be resting before a quiet dinner with my new daughter, sharing pleasant stories of our lives up to this point in time. We would spend tomorrow strolling along the seafront, feeding the seagulls perhaps and having a light lunch in the sunshine. Then on Friday, D-Day, I would say my goodbyes, wish her well and return to Brighton where I had to decide my pathway towards death. Now everything had been thrown up in the air, and I really, really needed it to land... soon.

"Henderson, what's got you so upset? As long as they think you're still in Bexhill, they won't need to go to Brighton to find you. Anyway, when they get their cash back from me, they'll be fine. Don't worry," she squeezed my shoulder as she smiled down at me.

I couldn't yet find the place that allowed me to speak, but I managed a nod.

She pulled her helmet over her head and shouted down at me, "Buckle up then, Seagull, it's time for you to meet some of The Seven!"

# CHAPTER 6

B ecky drove at a sedate pace this time, allowing me to pull myself together. I decided that once I had met her friends of the mysterious Seven, I would leave her in their care. This adventure I had strangely started to enjoy was becoming too unpredictable. She would not be alone and my job was done after all.

By the time we pulled up by the gates of a large park in the centre of town, I was almost back to my old self.

"Here we go," Becky said, as she dismounted. "We're a bit early, it's not quite dark yet. We only meet when the sun's gone down, it's safer. Do you fancy an ice cream?"

My tummy rumbled by way of reply, "Absolutely."

Becky took my bag and secured it in the sidecar by way of a handy cover that pulled out and locked over the top. The seafront was a short walk away, past Bexhill Museum the site of my first attempt to evade my pursuers. We arrived at a small café on the promenade. It was a squat, drab building, brightened by a rainbow collection of blow-up beach balls, shrimping nets and all sorts of other beach paraphernalia – most of which I couldn't identify.

"Do they have rum and raisin ice cream?" I asked.

"Nope, it's a choice of big one, little one, red sauce,

chocolate sauce, no sauce, flake or no flake."

"I see, big one with no sauce, please, but with a flake."

Becky ordered two ice cream cones and I insisted on paying. A father buying his daughter an ice cream at the seaside for the first time seemed like a rite of passage I should experience, even if she was thirty-three. We walked a short distance to a strikingly modern wooden beach shelter of sleek lines and unusual angles. I walked around it.

"Not your thing, eh?" Becky said, as she licked the red sauce running over the side of her cone. "Most of the oldies hate them."

"Not at all, it's magnificent. I noticed them earlier when I was on my way to your garage, they're an ingenious design." I sat beside her, picking the chocolate flake out of the whirl of vanilla ice cream.

"That surprises me."

"Don't forget furniture is my trade, it's not all restuffing old sofas, you know. What about you, have you always been interested in engineering and cars?"

"Pretty much. Mum spent most of my childhood moaning cos I always had something in bits, like the toaster or her sewing machine, but secretly I wanted to be an actress. I was in all the school plays, but she wanted me to have a real job."

"Well, that was sensible advice."

"Hm, I'm not so sure, most of the time I'm up to my ears in grease and debt. Tons of both."

"But being a mechanic is a skilled trade, surely? How have you got yourself in to debt, Becky?"

She shrugged, "Don't worry, I'll sort it, I always do."

We sat in companionable silence, watching a seagull pick apart a chip on the beach in front of us.

Becky turned to me with a smirk on her face, "What made you choose The Seagull as your codename? I mean, The Eagle or The Hawk, yes. But The Seagull?"

"I have no idea," I said, with a grin.

"Mind you, they're clever, you know, seagulls," Becky said. "They stamp their feet and pretend to be rain to make the worms come up."

"Is that true?"

"Apparently, it was on the telly. They can drink seawater too; they squirt the salt out of their eyes."

"No, that can't be true."

"Yeah, it was in the same programme. They've got a special gland or something."

"Well, every day's a school day, isn't it?"

"What did Maggie do?" Becky asked, out of the blue.

Just the mention of her name brought a weight back to my chest, and I needed a moment to force some air into my lungs, "Well, she was an illustrator. Children's books mostly, and also some very good history books. She had tremendous talent; authors loved her. Everyone loved her." I licked a melting lump of ice cream from the cone, "It's a shame no one illustrates crime novels. I read a lot of crime novels."

"I never got into reading," she said, licking her fingers again, having finished her ice cream. I offered her my handkerchief, "Oh, ta."

"That's a shame, Becky. I don't know what we'd do without books."

"I have one book at home."

I was horrified, "Just one?"

"Yep, couldn't do without it."

"Well, I suppose that's something. Please tell me it's a classic, at least."

"It depends how you define 'classic'. It's by Barbara Cartland." She laughed and stretched back on the seat, "It's under my armchair - it's got half a leg missing."

"Have you read it?"

"No."

"Good, leave it where it is," and we both laughed.

Time passed pleasantly, as the warm day drew to a close and the night arrived over the sea before us.

"We should go and find Adam," Becky said.

As we walked back to the park, I felt the need to be more prepared to meet this mysterious group she called The Seven, "Would this be a good time to tell me more about the people I'm about to meet?" I asked. "I assume there are seven of them?"

"We think so. We're only going to meet two though. Adam, who's number One, I'm Two and Callum is Three. We're pretty sure there's a Four, like us, but we're still working on that. Carl and Slim are Five and Six. We don't know who Seven is yet, he's the kingpin, but this Ellis might be it."

"Why is everyone a number?"

"It's what Adam called us all when he started to piece things together, he didn't know people's names just their phone numbers. Seven phones, seven people. Look, it's better if he explains it."

By this time, we had passed the familiar white façade of Bexhill Museum again and were back at the entrance to the park. She picked up the pace and we hurried past a sign that declared it as Egerton Park. I did my best to keep up with her, but I was tired and stumbled.

"Are you alright?" she asked, reaching a hand out for me. "It's probably only the moonlight, but you look very pale. Are you ill?"

"I'm fine," I lied, wanting to take her hand, but deciding pride was more important at this point. "As you said earlier, I need to get fit. Which way now?" I set off again, trying to look and sound hearty.

"It's this way," Becky said, indicating a path on the right that I had just marched past.

"Excellent," I said, with an about-turn and followed her across a swathe of grass towards what looked like a large boating pond in the distance.

Becky led me to a group of ancient oak trees, which cast shadows from the moonlight across a picnic bench at their centre.

"Hey," said a voice from the darkness.

"Hi," Becky said in return and chose a seat next to a dark figure already seated at the wooden table.

"Who are you?" the shadow said.

"Well, I'm..." I began, but Becky cut across me.

"He's an old friend of Mum's," she said. "He interrupted me and Carl today when we were getting into it about something."

I used my handkerchief to wipe the seat next to Becky, unsure what I was about to sit on in the dark, "My name is Henderson. Are you Callum or Adam?"

There was no reply from the shadow, but their face was suddenly illuminated by the opening of a laptop. It turned out that it was a youngish man, with lank, raven black hair, an underdeveloped beard and striking blue eyes, all cowled in a black hooded top. He began typing, his pencil-thin fingers flying across the keyboard.

"This is Adz," Becky said. "He's the one who figured out The Seven and brought us all together."

"You said he's got info. What?" Adam clearly liked to get straight to the point.

"Well," I began. "After the altercation between Carl and Becky about the money she had taken and shortly after I shot him, Carl mentioned the name Ellis," I paused as Adam stared at me, his mouth wide open.

"What money? And why the frigg did you shoot him?"

Becky shifted in her seat, "Right, yes, there are a few things in there I should explain."

"Too friggin' right!" he said.

Becky then gave him an impressive synopsis of our afternoon and evening so far, to which Adam listened in silence, while continuing to tap away on his laptop. The only salient fact she left out was our father-daughter relationship, but I understood that she may still be coming to terms with it herself and didn't want to bring that into the already quite complicated scenario.

"Jesus, Becky, what the hell were you doing skimming money off them?" he said. "I mean, there's never been guns before. You really must have... wait, WAIT," he shouted with a high-pitched yelp, and I wondered how recently his voice had broken. "Are you wearing a wire?" he yelled, managing to bring his pitch down to a more manly octave as he staggered up from the table.

"Me?" I said, reeling from his wild-eyed stare and shaking finger pointing at my face.

"Yes, you. Are you police?" his voice was lower, but his agitation formed spittle around his mouth.

"No, no, Adz, he's fine," Becky said.

He stabbed a bony digit at his laptop, "It says here there are three Hendersons in the Sussex police. I'm in their personnel records."

"It's not an uncommon name, but I'm an upholsterer not..."

"Shut it," he yelled, his pitch spiking again. "Strip. Take off your clothes!"

"I beg your pardon? Listen, young man, I came here to offer assistance, but I can easily leave ..."

"Take your friggin' clothes off NOW. Show me you aren't wearing a wire and recording all this," Adam shrieked, as he drew a small pen knife from the pocket of his sagging trousers.

Becky moved up beside me, attempting to sooth her irate friend, "Adz, there's no need for this. He's not police, honestly, I'd know."

Adam's face had taken on a demonic look, "We can't trust anyone, Becky, can't you see? It could be a trap,"

Becky sighed and turned to me, "Go on then, show him."

"I'm sorry, Becky, I know Adam is concerned for his safety, but he will simply have to accept my word."

"Not gonna happen," Adam said, moving the small knife around restlessly.

"For heaven's sake," I looked at Becky who simply shrugged - not a particularly helpful contribution, I thought. I tensed, knowing I was presented with little choice - I really needed to understand what on earth Becky was involved with before I felt comfortable enough to leave. Fine, if I had to do it, then it would be done with as much dignity as I could muster, "Becky, please turn away. Adam, remove that knife from my face or you will be seeing no proof of anything."

After a moment's hesitation, both complied with my instructions. I began with my shirt. Unbuttoning with shaky hands is not easy, but I tried not to show my fear or frustration. Once all the buttons were undone, I needed a moment to gather myself as my mind flashed back to the days of freezing schoolboy showers that had stripped away all confidence in my pasty body. I took a deep breath and held the shirt open to show Adam that no wires were hidden inside.

To my horror he made no reaction except to wave his pen knife at my trousers, indicating his requirement for their removal as well. I was ready to pack the whole thing in and walk away. Then I heard Becky's voice beside me, "Sorry," she said. One word only, but enough. A daughter's apology and appeal in a single word. She needed me to do this for her.

I clenched my jaw and looked Adam in the eye, "Very well. You will have your proof." I moved fast, unbuckled my belt, unzipped my corduroy trousers and pushed them down to my ankles. The night air was colder than I had anticipated on my bare flesh and I shivered. The fabric of my silk boxer shorts flapped lightly in the breeze.

I placed my hands boldly on my hips, "Is this what you wanted to see?" I said to Adam, and my heart nearly stopped beating as a large person emerged from behind a tree shining a bright light directly at me.

"Sorry," the person said, as the light moved up and down my body. "King Charles Cavalier?"

"Who the frigg' are you?" Adam said, hopping away from the light.

"I'm sorry," they said and the light went off. As my eyes adjusted back to the moonlight, I could see that it was in fact a large lady in a large t-shirt with a large purple dolphin leaping across her chest. She had wild hair of an indiscriminate colour amongst which sat a head torch, "I've lost my little Gina, she's a King Charles spaniel. She gets ever so giddy when there are squirrels, you see."

"No, we haven't seen your friggin' dog, now clear off!" Adam yelled, hitting a high note again.

"There's no need to be rude," she said, smoothing the dolphin over her ample bosom. "I'm sorry to interrupt your... well, enjoy your... evening," she said, before giving me what Maggie would have called an old-fashioned look and walking away into the darkness.

"Pull your trousers up, Henderson," Becky said. "We need to get on."

She settled back in her seat at the table, while Adam wiped his mouth of stress induced spittle and flopped in front of the laptop again.

"Do you have anything to say, Adam?" I asked, with barely supressed anger and humiliation, defiantly maintaining my pose with hands on hips and trousers round ankles. "I have exposed myself to you, to my... to Becky, and to half of Bexhill and you have nothing to say?"

"You're not wired, I get it," he said. "Can't be too careful though, can we?"

On the assumption that no actual apology would be forthcoming, I bent to retrieve my trousers and said, "Apparently not. Becky, I think we are wasting our time."

"Henderson, please," she said. "Adz, I'm sorry about taking the money, I didn't think. I'm going to give it back, but it's a good bargaining chip at the moment, isn't it?"

"I suppose," Adam said, now typing at extraordinary speed into his phone with just his thumbs. "On the other hand, it could get us all shot in the friggin' head. Where the hell is Callum? He hasn't replied to any of my texts for days."

"I haven't told Henderson anything about The Seven yet. Why don't you fill him in while we wait for Callum to get here. I really think he might be able to help us. Please, he's family... almost."

Adam put his phone away and sighed, "Fine, listen and don't talk, right."

"Of course, I wouldn't..." I stopped as his eyebrows rose up towards his greasy hairline. "Okay, go ahead."

Adam's gaze lowered to his laptop and he spoke quickly, while simultaneously typing and whizzing between various screens that flickered their reflection across his face, "As far as we can work out, there are seven people involved in a local, low level crime syndicate. Three run it – Carl, Slim and one other, probably the kingpin, maybe this Ellis bloke. Carl and Slim are too dumb to do it on their own. Then there's the three of us, who've been forced into it through blackmail. There's one more person we can't identify yet, but I'm pretty sure they're providing services like me, Becky and Callum, probably cos of blackmail as well. It's not very sophisticated, but it works. The idea was for none of us to know the others existed, which kept the risk to the top three minimal. WHAT?" the final word again shot up the scale to falsetto.

I had truly wanted to keep silent, but he was moving pretty fast and I needed some clarification, so had raised my hand, "May I speak?" I asked.

"You already have, go on," he snapped.

"Thank you. You called it a crime syndicate. I was concerned about what sort of crime we were talking about?"

It was Becky who answered, "Well, we definitely know that they sell drugs."

"Drugs! Good Lord."

"And they steal cars sometimes."

"Cars? That's appalling."

"There's probably other stuff, but that's all we know at

the moment," Adam replied, still engrossed in his screen.

"Sorry, Adam, but how do you know all this if their system is set up for no one within the group of seven to be aware of each other? Also, how do you know it's just seven people?"

Adam smirked into his laptop screen, "Because I'm clever. So clever I am going to find them and crucify them!"

# CHAPTER 7

In the blue light of the laptop's screen and framed by his black hood, Adam's face took on the look of a ghostly madman, "They don't know what they did when they dragged me and my sister into this, but they're going to pay. Big time!"

I decided that this was probably a good moment to follow his instructions and remain silent, as he sat hunched over the picnic table, his fists clenching open and shut, again and again.

"It was two years ago; out of nowhere I got this letter. No address, no nothing. It said: *We know what you did. Your sister is only where she is because you hacked her school exam results and upped her grades. What would happen if people found out?*

She got into university cos I hacked in and changed things, improved her grades and stuff. She's my big sister, right? What was I supposed to do? Now, she's got a big job in politics, a posh husband, kids – something like that could ruin her. Anyway, two weeks after the first letter I got another friggin' one, telling me to get seven untraceable pay-as-you-go phones and wait at the top of Galley Hill. I worked in a phone shop then, see. That's when I met Carl and Slim, they took six of the phones and left me with one. They said they'd be in contact and if I told anyone, my sister would be the one to suffer."

Adam fell silent. We waited, but after delivering coherent sentences for several minutes it appeared to have been too much, and he sat unmoving, not even blinking. I looked at Becky.

"They use Adz' hacking skills for all sorts of things," she said. "Changing drugs records, car reg information, all sorts. Don't know how he does it, but he's brilliant – unfortunately for him."

"And you?" I said, fearful of her response. "What do you do for them?"

"Cars. If a customer leaves their car with me overnight or the weekend, I drive it to the drug drops and courier the money or the gear. They're all anonymous old lady cars, so no one even looks twice at them. Then if they steal a car, I remove the VIN number and other stuff, change a few bits around so it's unrecognisable."

"I take it that you are the victim of blackmail too?"

"Yup, I don't know how they found out. It wasn't serious, not really. I got into a bit of debt – well, quite a bit of debt – last year. So, I faked a robbery at my flat to claim on insurance, just to help me get back on track. I made out all Mum's jewellery was taken; she had some nice stuff.

The police came to the house to have a look. I thought it would be straightforward; get a crime number, report it to the insurers, blah, blah. Anyway, this policeman noticed that my laptop was still on the kitchen table, mum's silver candlesticks on the side, one or two other things that hadn't been taken. I thought by only going for stuff like her jewellery it wouldn't be a huge thing.

Apparently, real burglars would have swiped the lot.

He was nice about it, seemed like a decent bloke, and said that it was unusual but not impossible for kids to break in and go for the quick, easy stuff like jewellery. Anyway, I put the claim in, hid the laptop and candlesticks when the insurance assessor came round, and boom - a big fat pay-out arrived. A week later I got a letter like Adz', threatening to dob me in for making a false claim. That's when it started."

I reached out and took her hand, "Whilst I can't support insurance fraud, you were clearly under a lot of pressure, Becky. I don't propose to say any more about it." If time allowed I would, however, have a quiet word with her about the necessity of careful budgeting, perhaps a short lesson on the benefits of spreadsheets too. "So, in short:

A. I'm being hunted to stop me speaking about what I witnessed.

B. You both need to get yourselves out from under the threat of blackmail.

And

C. We have to stop this crime spree across Bexhill.

What we need is a plan of action. What do you suggest, Adam?"

Breaking his gaze from the screen he looked at me, as if surprised that someone would ask his opinion. However, I was only being polite and didn't wait for a reply, "I think our best bet is to find out who Seven is," I continued.

"We're trying," he said, hunching back even lower over his keyboard.

"If we expose him, then we're equal."

"Yeah, I know that."

"We can identify him to the police and he can reveal your secrets, so it's stalemate. Bingo, they would be forced to stop their criminal activity," I concluded, just a little pleased with myself.

"Maybe," Adam said.

"I'm interested in how you found Becky, Adam? If you only had contact details for Carl and Slim."

"Before I gave them the phones, I made a note of all the numbers and ID's so I could track them. I monitored the texts, after a while it was obvious that Becky wasn't happy to be doing what they were asking."

"Of course she wasn't," I said and offered her a reassuring smile.

"So, I took the risk and sent her a message. It took a while to convince her, but we met a few weeks ago."

"That's when we really understood how they worked," Becky said. "Seven people, seven phones. Adam and me are numbers one and two. Then we got in touch with Callum via his phone – number three. After tracking his messages, it was obvious that he was doing stuff against his will. So, we got him on board. We reckon the person who has the fourth phone is being blackmailed too, but whoever it is won't respond to Adam's messages – probably too scared."

"I see," I said.

My problem-solving apparatus now in full swing, I began to pace around the ring of trees all thoughts of abandoning this adventure banished. It was obvious that

I couldn't leave Becky in the hands of Adam – the only option was for me to take control. I could almost hear Maggie cheering me on.

I pulled the little notebook from my pocket and extracted the pencil from within its spine, "So, we need to work out who number Seven is, agreed? Meanwhile, we should try to find out who Four is and bring them into our posse. Working together we have a much better chance of beating Carl, Slim and Seven. Let's begin with the one clue we seem to have regarding the top of the tree, the kingpin – the name, Ellis." I wrote *Ellis* across the top of a new page.

"Have you found many people called Ellis?" Becky asked Adam. "I suppose that's what you've been looking for?"

He nodded, "Yep, seventeen in Bexhill."

"From your conversations with him, can you tell whether he's old or young? Any distinguishing accents or speech defects?" I asked.

"Never spoke to him," Adam said. "He always texts."

Becky brandished her phone, "Same here."

I held out my hand to take a look at the texts for further clues, but she'd put it back into the pocket of her jeans, "It's all really anonymous stuff, he doesn't give anything away," she said.

"Are all seven phones the same?" I asked.

"Yeah, they were on offer," Adam said, drawing his phone out of his baggy pocket.

"Hm, well, at least they're distinctive," I said. "Being pink and having that kitten on the back."

"Hello, Kitty," Becky said.

I turned, expecting another visitor.

Becky giggled and pulled a face at Adam, "It's the name of the character, on the phone. It's called Hello Kitty. You can tell you don't have any children."

That smarted a bit, but I suppose it was reasonable. After all, I was starting out as a father rather late in life – hers and mine.

I returned to my point, "If we have to, we can work through all seventeen people called Ellis, but that might take far more time than is available to us," I was desperately trying to hold on to the leadership I had assumed, but was struggling to come up with a useful plan. I decided to buy myself a little time with another turn around the picnic table, "Let's think about this logically; some of the people called Ellis may well be children..."

"Nope," Adam said. "I'm in the electoral roll, from the council – both the open one and the one where people don't want their details given out. So, they have to be at least voting age."

"I see, good point, well done." As I rounded the table a large white building glowed above us at the top of the park and I pointed at it with my little pencil, "The museum!"

"What about it?" Becky said.

"Earlier today, when I was in the café, I saw Slim shouting into his phone, he didn't look happy – not unexpectedly in the circumstances. I took off this way and when I thought you were pursuing me as well, Becky,

I took shelter in the museum. There was a chap in there also on his mobile phone who was very suspicious. When he saw me, he overrode the ladies who were refusing me entry and told them to lock me inside. He had a strange look about him, but I don't remember seeing his phone and whether it was a pink kitty one. Might it have been Ellis?"

Adam sat back with a sigh, "Nope."

"How...? I've only just finished explaining what happened."

Adam pulled his hood closer around his greasy head, "You don't half friggin' go on, I got the gist ages ago. There's no Ellis on the museum staff list."

I suppose I should have admired his ingenuity, but something about this kid was getting under my skin, "I see, well, perhaps in future it would be worth listening to all the facts before haring off on your own. Discipline is one of the keys..."

Becky moved around to peer over Adam's shoulder, "Don't go on, Henderson."

Et tu Becky? Clearly family loyalty had not yet manifested itself in our relationship. However, I let it go as she pulled Adam's laptop towards her and he flinched when her hands touched his precious machine. I felt a little better.

"There's a photo of the staff here. Is he one of them?" she said.

I moved around to look at the page from the Bexhill Museum website. It appears that it was entirely run by volunteers and there amongst the group of somewhat elderly citizenry I recognised Beryl, Betty and the man with the lanyard, "That one," I said, pointing to him.

"Hm, back row, third from left," Becky said. "Denis Gordon, it says his name is. Damn, not Ellis. Mind you, Denis could sound a bit like Ellis. Are you sure you heard right?"

"Yes, he said it twice. Call Ellis."

"Where were you when he said it?" Adam asked, pulling the laptop back in front of him and using his sleeve to wipe where it had been touched.

"At the back of the garage - in the alley behind it, in fact."

In the moonlight I could see Becky's excitement, "I think there's something in this. You could have easily misheard from that distance. Carl was lying on the floor, almost under the car, groaning in pain. Denis, Ellis. Ellis, Denis."

"Yes, I see, perhaps you have a point. But I am almost certain..."

Adam looked at me, "*Almost* certain now, are you? Doesn't sound one hundred percent to me."

"Well, he was acting strangely towards me, his smile seemed false and uncomfortable. Perhaps he could be our man. Very well, it's our first possible lead, so we should pursue it." I wrote the name Denis Gordon in my notebook.

Adam watched me with a frown then went back to screen hopping, his fingers dancing across the keyboard, "Nothing coming up about him. No criminal record that I can find."

"That may not indicate his innocence; he hasn't been caught yet."

"Let's come back to the museum in the morning and check him out," Becky suggested.

"Very well, let us deal with Denis Gordon. Adam, you pursue the list of other people named Ellis, try and narrow it down on the assumption that I did in fact hear the correct name. Check they're all still alive or aren't over ninety, are still in the area and so on."

"K," was the mumbled reply, as I listed Adam's duties in my book.

"Now, what about Callum. Any news?" I asked.

"Nothing, he's been silent for about three days," Adam said, checking his phone.

I hesitated, "Now they've upped their game with guns and threats of violence, you don't think they've... done anything to him?"

Becky shook her head, "They wouldn't, would they? Have you intercepted any texts to his phone?"

"I've got them up here. One from Carl about four days ago, asking when the next delivery is due. He was a pharmacist in town somewhere and he used to get them drugs and stuff. After that, not a frigg."

"Let's hope that Callum is safe, but we should find out what's happening and why he's stopped communicating. We need more members of the circle on board, not less. So, I propose that tomorrow Becky and I pay him a visit, do you know where he lives?"

"Nope," Adam said.

"I'm pretty sure his is the chemists in Sackville Road, just round the corner."

"Good. So, let's reconvene tomorrow for a progress report." I angled the notebook to see the page in the moonlight, "To summarise our meeting; Adam will work on the list of people called Ellis and I also suggest you knuckle down and try to trace whoever has phone number Four. Becky and I have our tasks with Denis and Callum. Are we agreed?"

"Sounds good to me," Becky said.

"K," Adam said, before suddenly reaching out a skinny hand and ripping the little notebook from my grasp. "We don't want no records kept, either," he said, as he stood and flung the book with all his might through the trees and into the darkness. I stood in shock as we heard a tiny splash when the book hit the surface of the boating pond.

"That was our plan," I yelped, barely able to speak. "That was my little notebook. I had... I needed.... it was important."

"Tough," he said. "No records, no nothing to bring anything back to us."

"It's only a notebook," Becky said, giving me a small smile for what I took as an apology for her friend.

I stood beside the picnic table, thinking of all the lists now lost. Lists that had seen me through many tough months and offered some kind of anchor for the days ahead. Already I missed the weight of them in my pocket. I could feel my hands shaking again, like in the café earlier. My breathing was erratic. Then from the darkness I heard a voice, but couldn't make out what it said. I turned and peered through the trees, "Did you hear that?"

"What?" Becky said.

Then it came again, this time clearer, *"You can do it."* It was faint and seemed to come on a cool breath of air, but I knew the sound of Maggie's voice anywhere, *"You can do it.".* Could I really do it without my lists? Things were different now, after all, I was The Seagull. We were on the trail of criminals, out and out villains. I was the one leading the way. I had a purpose and perhaps I no longer needed my little book of lists. Previously, I wouldn't have considered participating in anything like this, I certainly had no history of it. But I was a father now and perhaps protecting my young was in my blood? Maybe I could do it.

Still a little shaky, I looked towards the pond as a shiver of excitement ran up and down my spine. I was freewheeling now, a whole new concept for me, but it was intoxicating.

I gripped my belt, hefted my trousers up under my tummy and looked at Adam, "Very well, let battle commence."

# CHAPTER 8

A short while later, Becky and I settled down in front of the beach hut with two mugs of tea, a bottle of tomato ketchup and two portions of cod and chips bought from Bertha's Plaice on the seafront. With a Strawberry Thief cushion underneath me, I was quite comfortable on the pebbles. Having shuffled from side to side the indentation in the stones cradled rather than needled my rear.

It was surprisingly warm for an English summer night and I was enjoying the food, with the waves gently toing and froing in front of me.

"Do they ever sleep?" I asked, looking up at a familiar looking seagull that circled above our heads.

"Yes, usually, but he can smell our chips. Or maybe it's the fish," she tore off a piece of her cod and threw it high into the air. The gull swooped and effortlessly took the fish in its beak. It did one more rather ostentatious loop, before gliding effortlessly away on the breeze.

"Maggie and I used to enjoy picnics. Not at the beach, but in the countryside. We would park next to a church in a tiny village called Jevington, then take our deckchairs and hamper up the hill through an avenue of conker trees."

"They sound like happy memories."

I wiped my fingers on a paper tissue, "Yes, they are. Very happy. We would sit on our deckchairs – funnily enough, I reupholstered them in Strawberry Thief fabric last summer – then we'd share a flask of tea and some egg sandwiches as we looked across the Sussex Downs. I always said they looked like upside-down puddings on a plate, which she loved, as an artist."

I found it hard to go on. The emptiness I'd experienced since Maggie's death had been like a huge anchor bound to my chest and I couldn't remove it. I hadn't been able to find a comfortable way to be without her.

We ate in silence until the last chips were gone, the greasy papers rolled-up and a few remaining scraps of batter thrown to our friend, the seagull, who had returned for second helpings.

Becky stretched out on the pebbles, "I used to have a specific star that I thought was Mum. I could see it from my window and I'd say goodnight to her every night. Do you believe people go to heaven, Henderson?"

"I'd like to think it exists, but I'm not a person of faith. I tend to only believe what can be seen or proven. So, no I can't believe that they do. Sadly, I think lives just end."

"You don't think Maggie is up there somewhere, waiting for you?"

"It's a lovely thought, but I really can't see how. Although I do dream of her sometimes sitting in her deckchair, with a cup of tea from the flask and an egg sandwich. When I wake up, I feel strangely comforted that I may be able to go there and find her soon, I mean, one day. But it's just a dream and reality settles back in when the black dog returns."

Becky sat up on her elbows, concern in her eyes, "I didn't know you had a dog. Have you left it at home?"

"If only that were possible," I said. "The black dog is a term for depression when you can't shake it off. It's like it's sitting beside you or on your lap the whole time."

The stones crunched as Becky settled down again, "Is that why you take pills?" she asked.

"Ah, you noticed."

"Yup."

"I did take pills for depression, but not any longer."

"What else is wrong with you then? Sorry, am I asking too many questions?"

"No, I imagine you are asking precisely the right number of questions for a daughter who has never met her father before. It's just that I haven't had too many people to talk to lately, so I'm a little out of practice. Maggie was the centre of attention for our friends, you see. It was always her that attracted a crowd, she was so... alive. When she went, they were attentive for a while, then they drifted away. I don't have the same appeal, I suppose."

"Your Mum must care about you, she always seems to be on the phone."

"Oh, yes, that's true enough. She does care, in her way, but I would never share too much with her, she would want to take over. I can't cope with that, not now." I gripped my hands tightly across my stomach, preparing myself. The words I was about to speak were new and I didn't know the affect they might have on either of us. I hadn't expected to say them here, but suddenly I wanted to, "Two weeks ago I was diagnosed with prostate cancer."

For a moment Becky didn't move, then I heard a tiny shift in the pebbles, "I'm sorry."

"I didn't want to tell you, because it's not fair - 'Hello, daughter, nice to meet you.' 'Goodbye, daughter, I'm about to die.'"

I kept my eyes on the distant sky above us, but I knew that Becky was looking at me, "There are treatments, though, aren't there?" she said. "Like chemo. It's not instant death, not these days."

"Yes, that's true. I'm scheduled to begin treatment on Monday, they say that with an operation and some aggressive chemotherapy I could have a chance of plodding on a bit longer."

"Is that why you need to be back on Friday, to get ready or something?"

"Yes," I lied.

"But they say you will survive?"

"Yes," I lied again.

"Hm," she said. "Good."

I tried to rise, but found that I had seized up and just rolled over, not unlike a beached whale, "Oof, oh dear... I appear, ouch..."

Becky leapt to her feet and crouched beside me pushing me upright. Somehow, I felt less embarrassed by my physical shortcomings with her now, and was able to grin and shake my head at my own inadequacies. Perhaps I had little dignity left to lose in front of her.

"Thank you," I puffed. "Beach life is a lot harder than I had imagined." I caught my breath and managed to stand before tottering over the shifting stones to the edge of the sea, where I turned back to her. "Now, I don't want you to concern yourself with my health. I realise, despite any shared DNA between us, I am a complete stranger to you. My intention in coming here was to honour Hazel's wishes and to provide you with answers to any questions you might have about your past. That's all."

Becky bit her lip and frowned at me, "That sounds pretty cold. Don't you want to get to know me? Maybe build a relationship with your daughter?"

"I see, yes, that's a very good point," I said. "I think I assumed that you wouldn't want a relationship with *me*. I wasn't sure I would make a particularly inspiring father figure. I had assumed that we would spend a couple of pleasant days together, then go our separate ways."

"You're probably right. Once this is all over, go back to Brighton and have your treatment." She stood for a moment in thought as if contemplating saying more, then made her way slowly back to the beach hut, pausing as she reached the little wooden terrace, "Can I ask? As a percentage, what chance did the doctors give you of survival?"

"They wouldn't commit. Fear of the culture of lawsuits, I suppose. They promised to do their best though." I failed to tell her that they and I both knew that their best would not ultimately be enough.

Becky considered this for a moment, "Okay," she said and went inside.

I feared that I may have rather spoiled the mood of the evening, so I collected the cushion and chip papers and hurried, as best I could, up the beach.

"I have to say that the food was delicious. One of the best fish suppers I've ever had," I said, attempting to bring some life back to the proceedings.

Becky was busy pulling what looked like bedding from inside the benches along one wall, "I should head off and find somewhere to stay this evening," I said. "Leave you to get some sleep."

"No need, you can stay here. Both benches turn into beds, you can have the one you used this afternoon," she said.

"But... but..." memories of the hard bed from earlier, followed by all sorts of other horrors, flashed before my eyes. "Where would we change for bed? How would we wash? I will need the bathroom several times during the night."

She shrugged, "There's a bucket for washing and the sea outside for other stuff. Who changes for bed anyway?"

"Good grief," I said. After talking about death so recently, I couldn't help but think that it seemed like an awfully good alternative to washing in a bucket and urinating in the sea. However, she was being kind and I felt it would be churlish to turn down her offer after the connection that was developing between us.

Becky hopped into bed, while I did my best to deal with

the bucket situation outside. Eventually, the sea and I also began our awkward new acquaintance. I changed into my pyjamas in the kitchen area behind Becky's head and took a few moments to unpack and hang my cream linen suit from a wooden beam in the ceiling of the hut. In the salt air most of the creases should fall away by morning.

I settled onto my wooden bed, "Goodnight, Becky. It's been very nice to get to know you today."

"Yep, you too," she said and switched off the battery-operated lantern that sat between us. "Sorry about all the trouble."

"Well, I wouldn't want you to tell anyone, but there is a part of me that's rather enjoying it. I am concerned that you seem prone to money troubles, though. The insurance claim cleared some debts, but you now need more money, which has led to guns and threats. Does the chap who owns the car business pay you enough? Should you ask for a pay rise?"

"I've tried that, but he's not interested. Jobs for female mechanics aren't easy to find, people still laugh when I tell them what I do."

"Well, that's ridiculous in this day and age."

"Tell me about it. Anyway, I'll get it sorted one way or the other. If not, I'll have to sell the flat. It was where I lived with mum and it's hard to think of someone else living there, but... oh well, we'll see."

"Well, if I can do anything, like working out a budget for you, then I'd be happy to help."

I heard her laugh, "A budget? Ok, thanks, I'll think about it."

"They're extremely useful tools, I…"

"Goodnight, Henderson."

I checked my watch on the hour, every hour through the night, but apart from the occasional short doze, I remained stubbornly awake. Eventually, as it approached five in the morning, I got up quietly, pulled the blanket around me, slipped on my shoes and tiptoed out onto the terrace.

I stretched my aching back and tried a few cursory knee bends. The sound of them cracking bounced across the empty beach and adjacent beach huts, so I sat instead. I spent some time enjoying the stars, marvelling as the pinpricks of ancient light sparkled in the vast emptiness above. I didn't mind feeling small as the sky stretched out in front of me, tucking itself neatly behind the distant horizon.

Soon I could see the early signs of sunrise in the east. Despite my weariness, the sky and the early light brought some peace to my aching body and tangled thoughts. For the first time in ages, it made me want to go on and see how long I could survive.

Then the old thoughts returned – survive? For what purpose? Wasn't it just delaying the inevitable? Wouldn't it be simpler to refuse treatment and fade away quietly?

Since my diagnosis I had found that it was not death itself that I was afraid of, it was all the fuss and bother in trying to prevent it that sent cold shivers up my spine. I even toyed with the idea of taking the time and method of departure into my own hands. I'd set myself the task of writing my final note, but couldn't find the right tone or words, so it went on the back burner as a bad idea.

As I sat in the glow of the morning light, I knew that having found a purpose in helping Becky and her friends, the pendulum was swinging towards trying to extend my life. Death and whatever came next – heaven, the hereafter or the long sleep - would have to wait a little longer.

It's funny to think that I had no idea how little that wait would actually be.

# CHAPTER 9

My Wednesday morning ablutions between the beach hut bucket and the sea were an experience I would not choose to repeat any time soon. The one saving grace was that my cream suit was wearable and once dressed I felt some level of renewed dignity.

Becky popped to a nearby shop and provided an excellent breakfast for us by lighting a small disposable barbeque and cooking bacon over the coals. We then set about devising a plan for our day of investigations. We decided to begin by working on Denis, who may be Ellis - who, in turn, may be Seven, the Kingpin. After he was ruled in or out, we would find out what had caused Callum to fall silent and see if murder was now a part of Seven's modus operandi. If so, a drastic recalculation of our approach would be required. However, for now, with chargrilled bacon rolls and a double dose of tablets inside me, I felt ready to begin the day's sleuthing.

Opposite the entrance to Bexhill Museum is a large block of flats, with excellent sea views and immaculate gardens partially surrounded by a well-trimmed laurel hedge. It was behind this foliage that Becky and I waited for the arrival of Denis.

"Just to be clear," I said, checking things off on my fingers in the absence of my little book of lists. "When we spot Denis, you will ring Seven's phone. If we hear it ring or he answers it, we know it's him. If nothing happens you will then send a text. If there is no reaction again, then he is unlikely to be Seven."

"Right, unless he's got his phone turned off," Becky said, from her position perched on her upturned helmet. "So, that's when we need to get a look at it and see if it's the same brand and style as ours. If it's a different model then he's in the clear."

"Did we decide how we were going to do that?"

"Not yet, we'll work it out later if we need to," Becky said, nonchalantly.

"I'd rather not leave too much to chance, if that's alright."

"Wait," she said, bouncing up and peering through the laurel leaves. "Someone's coming out."

I looked over her shoulder as the door to the museum opened and a plump woman in a floral skirt stepped out, with a large empty bread tray in her hands, "I assume that's not Denis?" Becky said, with a grin.

"That's Mrs A, she owns Café Amato just up the road. We had a lovely chat over a cheese scone when I first... good heavens! Yes, yes..." as the thought struck me, I stepped around the hedge and hurried towards the museum.

"Henderson, what are you playing at?" Becky called from behind me, but I was on a mission and could not be stopped.

"Mrs A! Good morning," I called, as I came up behind her.

The poor lady was taken completely by surprise and nearly fell back through the museum door with shock. As she turned and saw that it was me her fierce look brightened, "Henderson, you frightened me to death. What are you doing? I thought you were... I mean, the museum doesn't open until eleven."

"I was just passing. Do you work here as well as your café?"

"Sometimes, we do the catering for their events and things. I've just dropped off a finger lunch for the retired Rotarians," she turned and fought with a large bunch of keys to lock the museum doors.

"I just wanted to ask you a question, if I may?" I backed down the entrance ramp as she came towards me with her bread tray held in front of her like a jousting shield.

"Of course, we can chat while we walk to the café. There are some fresh cherry scones cooling even as we speak."

"They sound delicious, but I am rather tied up at the moment. Do you remember that I told you I was staying at the Sunnyside Guest House?"

"Well, yes, I think you did tell me. Don't you like it?"

"Oh, it's nothing like that, it's a lovely place. But I was wondering if you happened to mention to anyone that I was staying there?"

"I don't think so."

"Perhaps you were chatting to one of your other customers? Or a visitor wanted a recommendation of somewhere to stay and it was on your mind?"

"Well, now you come to mention it, there was a chap who came in just as you left in such a hurry yesterday. He said he thought he recognised you, maybe from school days. So, I said he might find you at Sunnyside up on South Cliff if he wanted to catch up with you."

"Bingo," I cried, clapping my hands. "Was it a very thin man or a very large man, or both?"

"No, no one like that..." she said, as I caught a glimpse of movement across the street and saw Becky waving her arms frantically above the laurel hedge. Keeping half my attention on Mrs A as she described the man who claimed to know me, I attempted to decipher Becky's signals, but had no idea what she was trying to convey.

"Well, thank you Mrs A, that's very useful," I stepped aside to let her continue her journey back to the café. "It was lovely to see you and I'm sure I'll be in for a scone again soon."

"Well, be quick, the cherry ones never hang around for long," she said and walked briskly up the road.

I turned and instantly bumped bellies with a tall man in a Bexhill Museum lanyard, that said 'DENIS' in block capitals. Ah, this was what Becky had been trying to tell me!

"Oh, you're here," I said, before I could stop myself.

Denis looked startled, "I beg your pardon?" Then he stepped back and took a proper look at me, "You again? I'm glad you came back. Have you come to see the model railway?"

He seemed very pleasant for a criminal kingpin, but the

new found sleuth in me was not so easily fooled. I threw a look across the road to Becky's hedge, but couldn't see her. I didn't know whether she had tried to ring his phone or send the text yet, so I needed to keep him talking, "Will Betty be here this morning?" was the first thing I thought of and it struck both him and me as a slightly odd question.

He frowned, "Do you know Betty?"

"No, no, not yet, but I thought it would be nice to see her again," I was making it sound even worse. To the relief of both of us his phone rang. Ah ha, I thought, got you! Denis pulled a large white phone from his pocket. It wasn't like the other phones at all, no pink kitty anywhere to be seen.

"I'm sorry, it's Beryl, I should take this," he said.

I left him to his call and crossed the road, promising to return later. As soon as I was out of his line of sight I changed direction and hopped back behind the hedge.

"I don't think Denis is either Ellis or Seven," I said. "He has a white phone, not like your ones, and nothing happened when you called Seven's phone. You did try and call, didn't you?"

"Yes, and text. Why did you run after that woman?" Becky asked.

"This is the interesting part. I was talking to her on Monday and I remembered that I told her I was staying at the Sunnyside. So, she is the only person who knew where I might be."

"You think she's Seven?"

"Good heavens, no. Her name is Mrs A – short for

Amato, not Ellis. She said that a man came in asking about me and she told him I was at Sunnyside! He must have been Seven, or at least connected to Carl and Slim in order to give them my location."

"Bingo!" Becky cried.

I looked at her, "That's exactly what I said!"

She shrugged, "Like father like daughter, they say. So, who was he?"

"She doesn't know his name, but she was able to describe him. She said that he was tall – taller than me. Lean – leaner than me. Middle aged – but younger than me (which stung a bit) - and may or may not have worn glasses." I felt elated to have gathered useful intelligence alongside eliminating Denis from our enquiries, and looked to Becky for some sort of recognition.

"Is that it?" she said, with a scowl. "It's not much to go on; a tallish, thinnish, middle-aged man who might wear glasses, but might not."

"Well, if you put it like that, it does sound a little... generic," I was deflating rapidly.

"So, we're no further on really. In fact, we've gone backwards, because we had a possible Seven in Denis, but now we have no one except Mr Average."

As my ego reached what I thought was its lowest point, The Ride of the Valkyries thundered from my jacket and I groaned.

"Good morning, Mother... You know where I am, I'm in Bexhill... Why do you want to know exactly where I am?... You're WHAT? Why on earth are you in Bexhill?... You are *not* on your holidays, you're checking up on me, or you want to force yourself on to Becky, or both!... No, I'm busy. We're both busy... Fine, fine. But it will have to be quick, we have something to do this afternoon... I'll ask her, but if she doesn't want to meet you, she doesn't have to... Very well, wait for us in Café Amato opposite the De La Warr Pavilion... It's the big theatre on the seafront... It's huge and white and Art Deco, you can't miss it... What?... Yes, my socks are dry. Goodbye."

"That didn't sound promising," Becky said, sitting back on her helmet.

"No. My mother has come to Bexhill for a few days holiday, which really means she wants to check up on me and meet her new granddaughter."

"Damn," Becky said.

I grimaced at her, "Indeed. I'm sorry, I'll meet her for a quick coffee and send her on her way before we find Callum."

"Nah, it's fine. I ought to meet her some time, I suppose. She sounds fun."

My mother has been called *fun* by my friends throughout my life and she was certainly unconventional, which was appealing to some. However, I would have preferred a little more convention and a lot less fun from her as I navigated my way through an anxious puberty.

"If you really want to meet her, please don't mention my diagnosis. I haven't told her yet."

"No, prob's. Anyway, this'll cheer you up," Becky said. "After I sent the random message to check out Denis, Seven just texted back."

"Oh, what did he say?"

Becky referred to her phone and read the message, "Stop playing around, Becky. If the gun won't bring you to order perhaps a criminal record will! You have ONE MORE CHANCE. There is a drop tonight. Bring the money to the usual meeting point. 6pm. Then we can start again."

"What does he mean by a criminal record?"

"Reporting me to the police, I suppose, for faking the robbery. It doesn't matter. The good news is that they'll be selling drugs somewhere tonight."

"How is that good news?"

"Cos, I can give them their money and get them off our backs."

"I see, I'll come with you to make sure they don't try anything awful. We may also be able to identify number Four, if they're providing services to them too."

"It could be a bit risky; they're hunting you, remember."

"Oh, yes, good point," I said, stepping closer to the hedge. "It does sound dangerous - going to a drugs den. But I can't let you go alone."

"It's not a den, the ones I've done before have been nice houses. Carl and Slim give me the gear – the drugs, and I drive it to the house and take the money back after it's all been sold."

"But whose houses are they?"

"Don't know, they're all empty ones up for sale."

"All of them? All up for sale?" I asked, light beginning to dawn for the second time this morning.

"Yes, I think so, why?"

"Are they all with the same estate agent?"

She hesitated, "Erm, maybe... no idea really."

"If they are then that's our connection to number Four; I bet the agent is being blackmailed to provide the locations for the drug transactions. It's a very clever arrangement if you think about it. Each time a different place, people coming and going under the guise of potential viewers." I was beginning to feel proud of my sleuthing skills again.

"Nice one, Seagull," Becky said.

I blushed, "Well, it's nothing really, just logical deduction, I suppose. Where's the meeting point?"

"The top of Galley Hill. It's where they always meet us."

"Where's Galley Hill?"

She began to check along the road to see if the coast was clear, "It's the highest point along this part of the coast. No sign of little and large, let's go."

We started across the road, "I assume it's isolated and quiet?" I asked.

"At night it is, it's the top of a cliff at the very end of the seafront before you get to Hastings. Apparently, smugglers used to use it as their look-out point."

"I see, then they've chosen an appropriate spot."

On the way to the café, I stopped to buy a straw hat from a souvenir shop by way of the beginnings of a disguise and to protect my already pink scalp from further sun damage. Feeling pleased with my new look, we approached Café Amato cautiously, in order to see if anyone appearing to be a giant or his skinny friend were inside. They were not, but what I saw sent an instinctive shudder through me – my mother, in the window, wildly waving a paper napkin at us.

# CHAPTER 10

"Thats straw will set off your eczema if you sweat into that hat," Mother said, as she kissed me on the cheek. "Natty though."

I quickly removed the hat, choosing to put my collar up instead, and slid down low in the seat opposite her, "Mother this is Becky. Becky this is..."

"Wait," she said, pulling Becky into the chair beside her. "I need a moment," and gently placed a finger in the centre of Becky's forehead.

"For heaven's sake, Mother..."

"Sshh."

Becky appeared too shocked to move, so I took a moment to note that Mother was in her typical summer attire; bare feet in purple glitter jelly sandals, pink leggings that ended above her slim ankles and a voluminous pale-green pinafore dress that hung loosely on her tiny frame. Around her neck dangled the usual citrine crystal, on the premise that it promoted good energy levels and mental clarity. This ensemble was all topped off by her snow-white hair. She always cut it herself with kitchen scissors and it sits in an uneven bowl shape around her head. Her eyes are extraordinarily green, made more so by a pair of large round glasses, with black frames and thick lenses.

Mother sat back and looked from me to Becky and back again, "What have you two been up to? Your auras are all to pot, they're all over the place."

Becky gripped her laminated menu to her chest, "What's she doing?"

Mother had taken hold of the crystal around her neck and was rubbing it frantically between the palms of her hands, as if trying to warm it, "Brown, grey... black," she mumbled to herself. "Hint of orange. Yes, orange. Layers, so many layers."

"Mother, behave, you're frightening Becky."

This seemed to snap her out of whatever trance she had put herself in, "Really? Me? Frightening? Not at all, dear. It's just that I'm good at assessing people's auras. A Yogini in Salamanca once told me that my sensitivity was huge, positively enormous."

"What the hell is an aura?" Becky said, pushing herself as far away from Mother as she could get.

I leant towards Becky, trying my best to sound reassuring, "An aura is believed to be an unseen spiritual energy that surrounds all living things. Those who think they can see it..." Mother huffed at this point, but I ignored her. "They say that the colour of your aura gives an insight into your emotional state or personality."

"We don't always see them, sometimes we simply feel them," Mother added, before turning to me. "What's up with you? Your energy is black today. Normally you're orange. Something's wrong, very wrong."

The cheerful presence of Mrs A arrived at just the right moment, "Hello, everyone. I hope you are hungry, it's my stew and dumplings special for lunch."

Mother stared at Mrs A, "Green... "

I slid lower still in my seat, "Mother, stop."

"Hm, very green - peaceful, healing... deceitful and jealous," Mother waved a hand vaguely at Mrs A. "It can go either way with the greens. I'll have carrot cake if you have some and it's not too heavy on the carrot. And cranberry juice," she sat back and concentrated her attention back on to me.

"Yes, of course... carrot cake," Mrs A clearly didn't know quite what had happened or what to do next.

"I should explain," I said, as I began my usual monologue, perfected over the years when out in Mother's company. "My Mother *thinks* she has psychic powers. She calls herself Psychic Sue..."

"It's my professional name," she said. "I sell clothes in a shop in Rye, I tell people I can match them to their auras. It's a bit of a gimmick really, but it works. You should pop in; I've got racks and racks of olives and sages that would suit you well. I go up to quite big sizes," she added unnecessarily, and Mrs A adjusted the elastic of her pleated skirt above her tummy.

"Yes, well, I don't get to Rye much," Mrs A said, with a pinched mouth. "One cranberry juice and one carrot cake, is that it?"

"One of your delicious cherry scones, please, if you have any left," I said, overcompensating.

A tight smile returned to her lips, "Thank you,

Henderson, of course. I have two left; can I tempt you to both?"

"Well, it's going to be a long day, so that would be lovely. And a nice cup of milky tea, please."

"I know how you like it, Henderson. And you... erm... madam?" she asked Becky.

"Just a black coffee, please," Becky said.

Mrs A disappeared behind the counter as Mother started to massage my hand, "I knew something was wrong. Your energy is black, it's never black."

"Black?" Becky asked.

"Mmmm," Mother said. "Lack of energy, illness..."

"Stop it," I pulled my hand away sharply, causing a pain to shoot up my arm. "Ouch."

"See! Black also means imminent death."

Becky gasped, "Really?"

Mother nodded, "Your aura doesn't lie... usually. Still, there's always a first time," she said, wiping the table enthusiastically with a paper napkin. "Now, let's get to know one another," and she shuffled her chair towards Becky. "I'm seventy-one. Howard is my only child. We tried for more, but your grandad was a quiet man..."

"He spent his life trying to get a word in when you took a breath," I said. My father had not been a huge influence in my life, always seeming to be content in the background, spending most of his time at work to ensure Mother had the life he thought she deserved. He left pretty much everything relating to me to Mother. Sometimes the only thing I think I inherited from him was his careful and constant list making. He was meticulous in his management of both the family finances and the organisation of the rare holidays we spent together when he took time away from work.

Mother continued, "Anyway, he died six years ago. You'd have liked him. I have fallen arches, all my own knees, but only one original hip. So, that's me."

Becky couldn't help but laugh, her fear clearly having now turned to fascination, which was not uncommon where Mother was concerned, "Fair enough. I'm a car mechanic, I've rebuilt my own vintage motorbike, I have all my own joints. I didn't know who my father was until yesterday and my mother died quite a while ago."

"I know, dear, I'm sorry. Hazel was a nice girl, if I remember. Wild, but house trained. Becky is short for Rebecca, isn't it? I'll call you Rebecca."

"No one calls me Rebecca."

"Good, that will make it special then - something only your granny calls you."

"It'll be more special if you call me Rebecca and I ignore you," Becky said, folding her arms tightly across her chest.

"I like her," Mother said to me, with a grin.

Mrs A returned at this point with our lunch. I began to butter a large, delicious smelling scone, which had the perfect crust on the top and a soft doughy centre full of chunks of sweet, scarlet cherries, "We can't stay long, Mother, we have things to do this afternoon. Where are you staying?"

"Same place as you, The Sunnyside Guest House."

"Oh, well, I've moved out of there."

"Why? She seems nice, Mary. She makes her own jams, you know."

"Yes, we do know that. There was a bit of trouble, that's all, so I stayed with Becky last night."

Mother's brows furrowed as she picked out flecks of carrot from her carrot cake, "What did you do?"

"Why do you assume I was the cause of the trouble?"

"Well, were you?"

I returned my focus to my scone, "Inadvertently."

"The thing is, Sue, we've got a little bit of a situation going on," Becky said, stirring a large spoonful of sugar into her coffee. "But we're sorting it."

"I guessed as much, I'm not Psychic Sue for nothing!"

"For the last time, you are not psychic, no such thing exists."

"Something's chasing you," she said, waving her carrot speckled fork at me. "You've got to find a way to escape it." She then pointed the fork towards Becky, "And you're responsible or something to do with it."

Becky stared at Mother for a moment, then smiled tightly, "Listen, Sue, do you really think that Henderson is about to die? Imminent death, you said."

"I hope not, I don't intend to bury my only child, I couldn't bear it. "

"But you said..."

"Well, auras probably have off-days too. Tell me what's going on, I can help."

"No," I said, at the same time Becky said, "Okay".

I sat back, trying my best to enjoy my cherry scone as Becky recounted our exploits over the last twenty-four hours. Mother seemed to grow taller than her five feet two inches as she took in the details of Carl's attack on Becky, the shooting of the gun, the meeting with Adam, the search for Seven and the other as yet unknown member of the circle, along with our fears for missing Callum. Finally, she let out a whistle, "That is quite a day or so you've been having. No wonder your auras are up the spout."

"So, you see why you need to pack your bags and head back to Rye first thing in the morning," I said. "I have quite enough to contend with without looking after you."

"Shush, Howard, you're going to need my help. We have to find Callum. What clues do we have?"

"We? Clues? Mother, please leave it."

"We don't know much," Becky said. "He seemed alright when he came to our first meeting. He said he was a pharmacist with a shop just around the corner. They were forcing him to provide drugs that they could sell. Morphine, other things I've never heard of that people get hooked on. Oh, and his wife is a vet, and they made him get some horse tranquilisers from her. It's called ketamine – Special K on the street. But his wife doesn't know about it, apparently. He wouldn't tell us what they were using to blackmail him, but he was very stressed out."

Becky had barely finished speaking before Mother was pulling her to her feet, "We need to know he's safe. Besides, if we are going to stand up to Seven, we need everyone on board... and Callum can get hold of tranquilizer darts, that sort of thing, if things turn nasty."

"Darts? Nothing will turn nasty... Mother, you're making me dizzy."

"Time for another tablet then," Becky said with a wink, as she pulled out a wallet from her back pocket.

Mother slung an enormous patchwork tote bag across her shoulders, "Tablet? What tablet does he need?"

"Nothing, just a paracetamol if he's feeling dizzy."

She began digging through the bag, "I've got some in here somewhere."

"I'm fine," I said, scowling at Becky.

"Henderson, I'm afraid I haven't got any money with me," she said, showing me her empty purse.

I could see that she was embarrassed and I thought of the debt problems that had drawn her into The Seven, "It's only a coffee, Becky. Don't worry, I'll get it."

I put some money on the table, as Mother emerged from her bag, "What was I looking for? Never mind, no time to waste," and she charged out of the café and onto the seafront.

"She's gone the wrong way," Becky said.

"She'll be back," I sighed. "She'll remember she doesn't know where she's going in a minute."

"Look, Henderson, I'm sorry, but I have to go and see my bank and sort out my account. They're threatening to cancel my overdraft and stuff."

"Becky, that's not good. May I ask, how much debt are you in?"

"Enough," she said and shrugged her shoulders. "Not your problem, it's down to me. Unless you fancy giving me back pay on thirty-odd years of pocket money?"

"Oh, well..."

"I'm kidding, I just need a couple of hours to sort it out."

"Becky, I would strongly advise you not to use the money you stole, that won't help the situation at all."

"I'm not that dumb," she said, running her hands through her steely grey hair. "I know I've got to give it back. I'll call you later. Will you be alright with Sue? You won't let her get you into trouble will you – you're on the run remember."

I put my straw hat back on and pulled the brim low over my eyebrows, "I haven't forgotten. Never fear, I have years of experience of managing my mother – memories of failing to do so as a child still haunt me, so I'm not about to let her run riot. You do what you need to do and I'll see what I can achieve here."

"Thanks, Henderson. Let me give you my number, in case you need me."

Becky tapped her pink kitty number into my phone and headed up the road towards the shops, just as Mother came marching back from the other direction, "Where's the chemist shop?" she yelled.

Becky turned, "Just up here."

Mother followed her with a battle cry, "Onwards!" and like a doomed foot soldier I fell in behind.

# CHAPTER 11

Ahead of me, Mother had already swung through the door of the chemist's shop and disappeared inside.

She was at the counter when I caught up, "Callum was so kind and ever so clever, for a pharmacist. I just wanted to thank him," she was saying to the assistant, a young girl with purple hair and a tattoo of a piglet on her neck.

"I'm sorry," she said, shifting awkwardly. "The thing is, we did write to everyone on our list, so I'm sorry you don't know."

"Know, dear? Know what?"

"Callum died, last week."

All the breath seemed to drop out of me and Mother leant on the counter in pretend or actual shock, "What a bombshell! How did it happen?"

The girl scratched her tattoo, "We're not allowed to say exactly what happened, the family... you know."

"I see, well, I'll send them flowers. I feel like I know them... his wife, Mrs... Mrs...?"

"Hall."

"Mrs Hall, yes. Poor woman! Where would I send the

flowers?"

"I'm not sure I can give you his home address."

"Well, he's dead, dear, so it's not really his home address any more, is it?"

The girl looked confused, "No, no, I suppose not."

"Just jot it down, that's it, nice clear writing. Lovely."

I opened the door and she started to back away from the assistant, "Such a sad day. Awful, but you've been very kind I shall remember to tell Callum when I see him," and she turned and charged past me on to the street.

She gave me the address with a frown, "So, he's dead. Murdered, do you think?"

I put my hands deep into my pockets to try and prevent them from shaking, "Now, Mother," I said. "We need to stay calm."

"I am calm," she replied.

"Why are you calm? There's a chance that Callum has been killed by The Seven or Seven or one of them, which means I am in even more danger than we'd thought."

"Imminent death," she said, with what I was sure was triumph in her voice. "The aura told me. But don't panic, he could have had a heart attack, or choked to death on a peanut. We need to find out what happened before we jump to any conclusions. Is his house far from here?"

I looked at the little scrap of paper and consulted the map function on my phone, "No, it's in the old town. It'll only take me five minutes in a taxi."

"Us. It'll only take *us* five minutes."

"Me."

"US. You need me now Becky's flounced off."

"She hasn't flounced anywhere, Mother. She had some financial matters to deal with, that's all. Go home, Mother, leave this to me," I was determined not to let her get any more involved. My new daughter and I were becoming quite a team and I didn't want her spoiling things.

The next moment the air was split by a blistering whistle, a sound I knew well from years of it shooting like an arrow across school playgrounds, to my constant shame. A taxi pulled up to the curb beside us and before I knew it, she was in the front passenger seat deep in conversation with the driver.

I settled into the back and we left the seafront behind us, crossed the town hall square and headed up into the wide, leafy streets of Bexhill's old town.

&#42; &#42; &#42;

"Very pretty," Mother said, as we stood outside a large old house, with high gables, dark beams and metal framed windows of ancient glass. "Now we're here and we know he's dead, what are we going to say?"

"Who are you?" a voice cut through the warm air. "If you're journalists you can sling your..."

"No, no, we're not journalists," I called up the path towards the house, unable to see the owner of the voice. "Erm... we're... from the library. Are you Mrs Hall?"

"Yes," the voice said. "What does the library want with me?"

I took a firm hold of the ornate iron gate for courage, "It's actually regarding your husband. We are very sorry for your loss, Mrs Hall."

A window banged and a few moments later the front door opened, and Mrs Hall appeared, "What's this about? If you're journalists, I swear I will call the police." She was a slim woman with long blonde hair wound in a haphazard pile on the top of her head.

"I'm sorry if we've interrupted you, Mrs Hall," I said, moving up the path. "I can assure you, we're not journalists. You see, your husband... your late husband, erm... had a number of outstanding library books and we are duty bound to retrieve them, I'm afraid."

"Are you sure you've got the right man?"

"Yes, indeed," I pulled out Hazel's letter that was still inside my jacket and pretended to consult the front of the envelope. "Mr Callum Hall, Pharmacist. Is that correct?"

"Yes, that's him," she said, taking off her glasses and cleaning them on the hem of her crumpled denim shirt. "To be honest, there was so much I didn't know about the toss-pot, this shouldn't be a surprise. You'd better come in." She stepped back allowing us into the hallway

It was a pleasant space, large by usual standards, with light flooding down on us from a stained-glass window above the stairs. Mrs Hall pointed vaguely to a room behind her, "Help yourself, all his stuff is in there," and she disappeared through a door to our left.

We moved quickly into Callum's study, a small room, with a modern desk, filing cabinets and a wall lined with bookshelves.

Mother closed the door quietly behind her, "What are we going to do in here? We need to talk to her, not hide in his study?"

I began to silently and methodically open each of the drawers in the desk, "I thought we should probably try and find his phone – each member of The Seven has their own. If Mrs Hall finds it, she might get involved and put herself in danger. Worse still she could go to the authorities and scupper everything."

Mother moved quickly to the filing cabinets, "Not bad, Howard, not bad at all. Nothing in this one... or this one, just files and papers."

"Nothing here either, let's check the shelves."

After a thorough search, we found nothing, "Perhaps whoever killed him took the phone?" I said, looking around for any further hiding places.

"I'll call for it," Mother said, pulling at the crystal around her neck.

"You are not going to find a mobile phone with that inanimate lump of rock, don't be ridiculous."

She ignored me and started walking slowly around the room, rubbing the crystal incessantly until the leather string that held it in place snapped and it fell to the floor.

"Blast," Mother said and knelt down to retrieve it from under the desk.

"Leave it, we don't have time."

"Hang on, Howard... the phone's here!" she was bent right over with her head on the floor looking under the desk. She tore away some tape that held the phone on the underside of the desk drawer and handed it up to me.

"Good work," I said, checking that the little pink kitty was on the back, which indeed it was. I tapped the screen, "It's not locked, thank goodness."

"Do you still think the crystal is just a piece of rock?" Mother said, climbing back to her feet. "It led me straight to the phone."

I ignored her, "Let's find out how he died, then get out of here."

I headed into the hallway and knocked on the door to what I assumed was the front room, "Mrs Hall, may we come in?"

"Whatever," came the reply.

I opened the door and found Mrs Hall curled up in a large wing-back arm chair in an elegant, airy living room.

"I'm afraid we've had no luck with the books," I said.

"Probably in his other house, then," she said, before throwing back a slug of what looked like brandy in a rather large glass.

"Other house?"

"With his other family."

"Do you mean that Callum was...?"

"Yup, leading a full-on lying other life. He was a conniving, two-faced, great big, stinking, bigamist!" she sniffed and stared deeply into her glass. "It must have been bloody exhausting keeping two families on the go, no wonder he was stressed all the time. It all got too much, I suppose, and he walked into the sea – not here, oh no, that would have been too convenient. He did it in Whitby, where his other life was. Calmly walked into the bloody water, apparently. He had the guts to do that, but not to tell either of his wives the truth," she started to clean her glasses again so aggressively that I worried for the delicate frames.

"You poor thing," Mother said, plonking herself on the footstool next to Mrs Hall's chair. "Now, are you sure he didn't get pushed into the water? He did walk in?"

"There was a witness. They said he took his shoes and socks off, rolled up his trousers and just kept walking until he disappeared into the waves." Mrs Hall laughed, "They thought he was going for a paddle."

Mother nodded and laid her hand gently on Mrs Hall's knee, "You'll be fine, love. Better off without him, by the sounds of it. At least you have your own career, being a vet's a lovely job, I expect."

Mrs Hall stared at her, tears welling in her red rimmed eyes, "I'm not a vet! That was her, his other... how did you know that?"

Mother shot a look at me, "Erm, well..."

"She's psychic," I said.

"Yes, yes, I am. I saw a horse's hooves and a syringe, you see..."

I put a steadying hand on Mother's shoulder, "Perhaps it's time we left."

* * *

Once we were out of sight of the house, I leant against a fence, fanning myself with my hat.

"So, he wasn't murdered after all. Suicide, that's good,

isn't it?" Mother said, sifting through the contents of her tote bag.

"I wouldn't call it *good*."

"Well, it's good for you. They haven't started murdering people yet, so you might just get beaten up or a kneecap blown off."

"Mother, how is that helpful?"

She pulled out a packet of mints from her bag, "Mint? You look like you need some sugar, you're a bit pale."

"I'm fine," I said, straightening my back.

"Good lying, by the way. I never thought you would be so devious."

"What do you mean?"

"The library books, good work, son. There's hope for you yet."

I felt a warmth bubble up inside my chest, "Thank you." Before things got too pleasant between us, I noticed a sign on the fence beside me, "Oh, look, this is a bed and breakfast. I might just pop in and see if they have a room for a couple of nights."

"I think you'll need a few more than a couple, it might take a while to sort this lot out."

"I intend to wrap it all up by Friday morning at the latest, I need to be home by then," I said, with renewed confidence, as I walked up the honeysuckle-scented path.

"Why?"

"None of your business."

Mother was still sulking when I returned ten minutes

later, having secured a pleasant room for the next two nights, with an ensuite bathroom rather than a big blue bucket and the English Channel.

"What's so special about Friday?" she said, arms folded.

"I told you, it's none of your business," I had learnt many years ago that the blunt approach is always better with Mother.

"Hmph. What child keeps secrets from their mother?"

"All of them," I said, waving at a taxi that was drawing up in front of us. "I asked the chap in the B&B to order a taxi to drop you back at Sunnyside and then take me on to meet Becky."

"Where are you meeting her?"

"Somewhere you can't find us. I need you to sit tight in the guest house for now, the next task is one for me and Becky alone."

She protested all the way back to South Cliff and was still going when I bundled her out of the car and instructed the driver to drive on. He wasn't entirely happy accelerating with an old lady still hanging on to the door handle, but I insisted. Once we shook her off, we took a detour to a café that served takeaway lunches and he received a sizeable tip for his troubles.

I enjoyed my salmon sandwich and potato wedges outside the Lazy Dayz Beach Hut, and spent some time watching families build sand castles and scream as the seagulls swooped low over their heads. Despite the growing pain around my hips and back, life seemed good... for now. Bumping into the awful reality of Callum's suicide had made me certain that it was not the path for me, meaning one less option to consider on Friday.

Soon the warmth of the sun and idle chatter of children sent me off into a comfortable doze, until the tell-tale rumble of an old engine woke me.

When I had filled Becky in on our morning's discoveries she snorted, "Suicide? So that's where Callum went. Serves him right by the sounds of it."

"That a little harsh. The additional pressure from Seven to provide the drugs must have caused him to take drastic action, leaving children without their father."

She gave one of her shrugs, "It happens," and I felt the barb land firmly in my chest.

"Yes, of course. How about you? Did you get things sorted with the bank?"

"Not really," she tossed her helmet in the air and caught it deftly. "I need a sudden injection of cash, maybe I'll buy a lottery ticket. But we won't let it grind us down. We need to get going."

Becky pulled out her keys and opened the hut, disappearing inside for a moment before returning with her rucksack containing Seven's stolen money, "Time to go."

"But shouldn't we talk about your money situation?"

"Not unless you've got a few spare thousand hanging around," she said, walking back around the hut. "I need to meet Carl and Slim. You up for it?"

"Yes, of course."

Twenty minutes later, I was hidden in a large gorse

bush half way up Galley Hill. It was a steep climb from there to where Becky was talking to Carl. I couldn't hear the conversation, but it didn't last long. She handed over the rucksack, Carl checked its contents and nodded at her. He then opened the boot of his car and pulled out an old-fashioned tan briefcase. She snatched the bag from him and came back down the hill towards me.

"Get back to the bike," she hissed, as she marched past me.

I backed out of the bush, "What did he say?"

"Just the usual rubbish. They've got their money back, but they want you too. I told them you'd vanished, so they'll just have to suck it up."

"Does that mean they'll stop looking for me?"

"I doubt it, but it might buy us a bit of time. No point worrying about that now, we need to get to the drop point. It's one of the massive houses off Cooden Drive. We've got some drug running to do!"

# CHAPTER 12

Becky was not wrong, the house in question was huge. The sleek, white building had a circular drive, but today, instead of cars, there was a steady stream of people walking up it.

"It's all a bit obvious, isn't it?" I said. "In broad daylight, just filing in to collect drugs. Although, I have to say they're not exactly what I had in mind when I was thinking of drug addicts."

Becky pointed to a sign that had been set up at the bottom of the drive:

'For Sale

Open Viewing today

6pm to 7pm'

"Oh, I see. Are these people house buyers or addicts?"

"Both. Either. You'd be surprised who's addicted to what these days. Loads of oldies get hooked on prescription drugs their GP won't prescribe anymore. I need to go and sort this lot out," she said, as she took the briefcase I had been holding in the sidecar. "You go inside and see what you can find out about the estate agent, see if they're one of us. I'll meet you back here in a little while."

"Are you sure you'll be okay on your own?"

"No problem, I've done it loads of times before."

Becky quickly disappeared around the side of the house and through a gate. I donned my straw hat, brushed down my crumpled suit and tried to look like a prospective home buyer as I strolled up the drive.

The inside of the house was just as impressive as the outside. Large, white walls rose to meet high ceilings, enormous canvases hung in strategically lit spaces with slap-dash strokes of primary colours thrown across them. Well-dressed couples moved smoothly around the rooms, referring to glossy sales brochures and pointing out flaws that might allow for negotiation on the price.

"Good evening," a soft voice said from behind me.

I looked over my shoulder to see a woman of about my height, with a bold afro like a halo that framed her delicate face and strong, professional smile, "I'm Destiny, the estate agent for this property." She held out her hand and, as I looked down to take it, I saw that she was heavily pregnant.

My blank expression must have taken her by surprise, as her smile slipped and a shadow crossed her face, "Are you here for the viewing or...?"

So, she knew what else was going on here, "Yes, I am. For the viewing. Yes."

Destiny's professional smile returned, "Excellent. Perhaps I could make a note of your details, for our records?"

"Yes, of course."

"Your name?"

That question shouldn't have foxed me, but it did, as a new thought popped into my head. My stomach lurched and my bladder shifted – was I looking into the eyes of Seven? I had assumed that he was a kingpin, but he could just as easily be a queen! Good grief, did we need to rethink our assessment of Ellis, could it be *Mrs* Ellis?

I removed my hat and wiped my damp brow with my hanky, buying for time, "Erm, sorry, I didn't quite catch your name. Destiny, was it? Destiny Ellis?"

"No, Destiny Holmes. I work for Holmes for Better Homes. It's a bit of a mouthful, but at least people seem to remember it," she said. "What exactly are you looking for? Something in this specific area, of this size?"

"Yes, yes, something like this," I said, waving my hat vaguely around. "Maybe bigger, hard to tell. Sorry, is that my...? One moment..." I reached into my jacket pocket ostentatiously and withdrew Callum's pink kitty phone, my eyes never leaving her face. As she saw the phone she flinched slightly, it was very quick, but I saw it. Bingo! But was it because she was Seven, or because she had been given one of these phones when she was drawn into the circle?

"Destiny, I think we should talk."

"Really? About what?" she was instantly on edge.

"Perhaps we could go into the garden?"

She took a step backwards, "No, thank you, I'm afraid I have other clients to talk to." She clutched her pile of brochures and hurried away.

I quickly located Callum's texts and scrolled through

until I found what were clearly messages from Seven, demanding more 'goods' from him. I typed a brief reply, Is this you?

I set off in pursuit of Destiny as she chatted to a young couple by an extraordinary glass and steel fireplace. I stood as close as I could and hit send, but heard no tell-tale sound from the handbag hanging from her shoulder to notify her of the text's arrival.

"Well, feel free to have a look round upstairs, there is an awful lot to see," she said and turned, narrowly missing bumping into me. "Oh, what are you doing?"

"Erm, well, I just sent you a message. I wanted to check you received it?"

"Why would you do that?"

"Would you mind checking?"

"Yes, I would mind. What's the matter with you?"

"Destiny, blackmail is an awful business... please check your phone," I surprised myself with the sternness of my demand, but it had the desired effect.

She swallowed hard, placed her brochures on the armchair beside us and opened her handbag. I could see her hand shaking slightly as she pulled out a slim phone with a diamante encrusted cover, it was far too big.

"Not that one," I said, with as much menace as I could muster. "The pink one, with the kitten on the back."

Her eyes flashed to the left and right, looking for options for escape, but I had managed, albeit inadvertently, to back her into a corner. Slowly, she replaced her sparkling phone and hesitated before withdrawing the familiar small pink one.

"Now, check for a message," I instructed.

Her hands were really shaking now, as she fumbled with the screen, "I don't understand. Why are you here? I'm doing what I'm told, aren't I? Someone's here doing... whatever they do."

She seemed totally genuine in her fear and innocence, but I had to be sure, "Let me see, please." I took the phone from her and was relieved to see that there were no new texts and breathed a huge sigh of relief, "Thank goodness." I really wouldn't have known what to do if she had been Seven, "I'm sorry to have upset you, but I had to be sure. Destiny, my name is Henderson and I'm here to help you."

"Help me? How? Why?"

"I'm on your side, I'm trying to stop all this. There are others like you, being forced to be a part of it."

"Others? What others?"

"There are seven of these phones. Three belong to the gang who are in charge. We believe that four are with people like you, people who have been drawn into crime against their will."

She stood quite still and I could see that she was weighing up whether to trust me or not.

"Destiny, my daughter is trapped like you. Her name is Becky, they make her bring the drugs to your houses, but she's being blackmailed into working for them. If she doesn't do as they ask, they say they'll reveal her secrets to the police."

Destiny shook her head slowly, "I thought I was alone."

I took her hand, which was still trembling, "Oh, you are

not alone, Destiny, not now."

She looked around and then moved me through the large glass doors and out on to the veranda that ran the width of the back of the house, "I can't believe that there are others like me."

"Becky and her friend, Adam, have been trying to contact you. Didn't you get Adam's messages?"

"I don't think so, no one uses their names."

"I assume you're forced to let them piggyback their drugs sales onto your house viewings?"

"Yes, exactly. Every time I get an empty house, I have to let them know. These people live in Dubai most of the time. It's ridiculous, I'm married to a vicar for God's sake," she leant heavily against the stone work.

"Yes, I can see that's going to be awkward for you. May I ask what hold they have over you?"

Destiny paused and looked carefully at me, "I can't say. It was all such a long time ago and I've put it behind me. My husband, Mark, can't know that I've lied to him for so many years, it could end our marriage. Besides, it's taken so long for people to accept me and this would ruin everything. I thought I'd paid the price before, now I'm paying it again," tears began to fall unchecked down her cheeks.

"Is it that bad? Would your husband really abandon you with..." I pointed to the obvious bump under her cream dress.

"I don't know, maybe," her hands caressed her swollen stomach with a soft circling motion, comforting herself and the little one. "He's a good man, too good for me."

The poor woman looked defeated and I took a reassuring grip of her elbow, "We'll get you out of this, please don't distress yourself. We're trying to identify the leader of the group – we call him Seven, as he's the holder of the seventh phone. I assume you receive messages from him with your instructions? Can you give us any clues about him... or her, from the messages?"

"No, it's always really straightforward, polite even. What do you want me to do? I have to be careful; this is Mark's father's business; they can't know anything."

"Leave it to us," I said. "We'll get to the bottom of it. Don't do anything differently, they mustn't get suspicious. When we've worked it all out, we'll all come together and bring this to an end. We'll send you a message on the kitty phone, I'll sign it with my code name, so you know it's me – The Seagull."

"The Seagull?"

"It's a long story. I'll need your number."

"Right, this is so amazing," she said, wiping the tears from her face. She took my phone from me and programmed in her kitty phone number. "Henderson, you don't know how relieved I am this will all come to an end," she reached out and pulled me into a hug. I wasn't a great hugger, so I took a moment to settle in, but when I did it was really rather lovely.

"It wasn't bad, what I did," she whispered in my ear. "I just want you to know that. But I went to prison..." she pulled back and stuck her hands on her hips. "Oh, what the hell. Look, a long time ago I stole some credit cards and used them to buy all sorts of things. I lived a whole fictional life on other people's money, until... until I got pregnant. I was just a kid, how could I cope with a child? A friend said she knew someone who could get rid of it, but they botched it. I ended up in hospital, the police got involved and everything came out. I lost the baby and spent time in prison. When I got out I was determined to start again, so I made up another history for myself and moved here to start a new life, but this time I didn't steal to do it. When I met Mark, he was so gentle, so kind and took me for exactly who I was. I meant to tell him about the real me, all I'd done in the past, but I was too afraid of losing him. So, I kept quiet and before long it was too late to go back. Then we got married and now this... this baby. I didn't think I could have any more children, after... well, this is my second chance, it's such a blessing. I can't lose it all, I just can't. I'm not a bad person."

She took a deep breath and wiped her damp cheeks, "Sorry, I've never told that to anyone before."

"Well, you obviously needed to say it. Does it feel better?"

She gave me a weak smile, "It does, it feels a lot better."

"I can't imagine what you went through, but you paid your debt. You were young, surely a man of the cloth would understand."

"Maybe, if I'd been brave enough to tell him right at the beginning. No secrets, he said. How could he trust me again if he realised that I'm not the woman he thought he'd married?"

"I think you might be underestimating him. He's a vicar, I mean, he should be able to forgive a sin of the past, surely? I don't know much about religion, but I'm pretty sure that's how it should work."

"In theory, yes, but when you get hurt even vicars find it hard not be human. Since I got the letter threatening to tell him about me, I've been so scared. I have everything I ever wanted," she looked at me intently. "Get me out of this, Henderson. Please."

I stood a little taller and straightened my back, "I will do my best, Destiny. I think we have them on the ropes and I hope the end is nigh." I was proud of my little biblical quip, but felt even better that I could be useful.

"Thank you," she said, just as an older couple made their way out onto the veranda.

"Do you need to talk to these people?"

She looked over her shoulder, "No, I don't think they're here for me."

"Really?" I watched the couple help each other down the steps and onto the grass. They walked carefully across the lawn, stopping every few paces and checking around them with nervous looks. Luckily, Destiny and I were tucked behind the bay tree and couldn't be seen.

"I must go," Destiny said in my ear. "Thank you, Henderson," and she kissed me lightly on the cheek before returning to the house.

I peered around the bay tree to follow the progress of the old couple. They made their hesitant way towards a large summer house at the bottom of the garden, and with one final glance around them they disappeared behind it. I crept down the steps and started across the lawn. Half way to the summer house a strange tingle at the back of my neck made me shiver as if a shadow had passed over me, the Henderson Niggle. I looked back to see the giant figure of Slim standing in the middle of the glass windows leering at me with a hungry grin, as if he had spied a decent sized supper.

# CHAPTER 13

My bladder took a turn for the worse at the sight of Slim. I was pretty sure I didn't possess the wherewithal to fight a small man, let alone an enormous one like Slim. With this in mind, I turned tail and set off at a gallop towards the bottom of the garden.

It was quickly apparent that this had been a mistake, as the lawn ended abruptly at the edge of a cliff – not something included in the glossy sales brochures, I would imagine.

I turned again and headed back up the garden, Slim watching me lumber about with a grin on his face. He unfolded his arms and I darted around to the side of the house just as Carl came through the wooden side gate ahead of me. I caught a sunny glint from his glasses as he looked directly at me. I was trapped.

I gave my trousers a healthy heave under my stomach and headed back to the veranda and up the steps, sensing that Carl was closing in behind me.

Slim retreated to the centre of the open windows like an oversized goalie, but I saw a small opening on either side of him. In an instant a plan appeared; I feigned a slight turn to my left, Slim followed suit, but at the last moment I changed course and headed to my right. As I suspected, he was too slow to pick up on my subterfuge and I slipped past him.

In the instant I thought I was clear, Slim showed that he was more agile than I had anticipated and stuck out his leg catching my back foot, sending me tumbling forwards. I took a few exaggerated steps, like an over enthusiastic Irish jig, but I knew that gravity plus speed was taking me down.

I sprawled across the expensive rug, plunging nose first into its deep pile. However, adrenaline drove me on and I rolled onto my back and began crawling away, as a crab would scurry back to the safety of the surf. I cleared the rug and managed to twist until I could hold the edge of it in both hands and pulled with all my might. Although it didn't shift very far, it was enough to unbalance Slim who was advancing on me. He began to sway, first forwards then back. I gave another heave and quite literally pulled the rug from under him. I managed to take him far enough backwards that he couldn't stop the momentum of his weight tipping him over. I watched in relief as he went down, taking Carl with him. As they hit the floor in an untidy heap, I rose and limped stiffly past a small audience of transfixed house buyers, tipped my straw hat to Destiny and shot out of the front door.

As I reached the pavement, I heard a bellow behind me and turned to see Carl and Slim fighting with each other to get through the door. Their determination to snatch their prey at last had clearly led to a quick recovery. I turned towards the town and dashed off as fast as I could, my abject terror overcoming the lack of sprinter's grace or physique.

Every few steps I checked the progress of my pursuers. Slim was falling behind, but Carl seemed to be gaining ground with his younger, thinner legs moving faster than my own. It was clear I couldn't out run him. As I turned a corner I saw a front garden on a grand scale brimming with what Maggie would have enjoyed as 'fabulous tat', but at this moment I recalibrated it as opportunity.

I careered through the gate and threw myself behind possibly the ugliest garden bench I had ever seen - every inch covered with sea shells. As I crouched panting behind it, I heard Carl pass the end of the garden, but then his footsteps halted. The road I had turned into was long and wide and it must have been clear that I was not ahead of him.

It was only a matter of time before he found my hiding place, I needed another plan. I peered around the bench at an ornamental shell-covered windmill, a fake frog infested pond over which a shell-encrusted bridge stretched. There was every form of useless garden decoration slathered in sea shells and pebbles, to the point that I wondered why the local beaches weren't completely bare, but nothing that looked like a way of escape.

I heard the creak of the garden gate, this was it. I was about to be captured and most probably silenced - at the very least my kneecaps were in for a rude awakening. The last time I thought I had nowhere to turn I was prepared for my fate, but now I wanted to fight. I wanted to fight on for Becky, for Destiny, maybe even for Adam and most certainly for myself.

Without thinking I rose from my hiding place and screamed at full force, "BINGO!!!"

Apparently, I was sufficiently startling for Carl to freeze in front of me, giving me the precious seconds required to hop over the shell bridge and make a lunge for the little shell windmill. Grabbing one of the encrusted sails, I ripped it away and flung it at Carl. Without waiting for it to connect, I tore off another sail and threw that, then another.

Carl stood laughing at me, as the sails landed uselessly around the garden, none having made contact. As he laughed an anger welled up in me, born of years of being mocked by other, fitter, sportier children, by my mother as I refused to jump in puddles for fun, by our friends giggling at tales of my dodgy feet causing me to keel over at inopportune moments. With every ounce of energy and anger I possessed, I let the fourth and final shell-covered sail fly.

It bounced off the already bruised side of Carl's head with a thud. He blinked, then without a change of expression sank to his knees and fell forwards onto his face.

I immediately began to panic that I might actually have killed Carl this time, as Slim appeared at the garden gate. Distressed to see his accomplice face down in the shallow pond, he stumbled forward and pulled the unconscious Carl dripping from the green water, "Speak to me, Carl. Speak to me."

I tiptoed back over the bridge and past him unnoticed, as Becky and her motorbike chugged to a halt in the road. She revved the engine and dragged me round the bike with one hand, pulling me unceremoniously into the sidecar. I had no time to step inside, but fell in bottom first my knees folding up to my chin, as Becky powered the bike away.

* * *

It was several hours later that I felt sufficiently recovered to join Becky, Adam and Mother around the picnic table in the depths of a dark Egerton Park.

"How did they know you were at the house?" Mother asked, rubbing my back.

"Do stop stroking me, Mother."

"They probably just got lucky," Becky said. "Sometimes they come and check up on how things are going. It was just unlucky you were there."

"Unlucky for all of us," Adam said, rubbing his sparse beard. "Becky's dropped herself right in it, hasn't she? Like a friggin' moron."

"Oy," Becky said. "He needed saving, what was I supposed to do, drive off and leave him?"

"Yep, cos now they know that you're working together. So, they're going to be looking for *both* of you. It's a friggin' disaster."

Mother nodded, causing her glasses to slide to the end of her nose, "He's got a point, you should have left him to fend for himself, Becky. From the sounds of it he was doing all right. But I think you had better pop round in the morning, Howard, and apologise to the people in the shell house and pay for the damage."

"Mother, for goodness sake."

Becky leaned into the table, "Well, it's too late now. I've had messages from Carl and Seven all evening. I've turned my phone off, but we need to move quickly or get out of town fast. The money I took tonight won't get us far, but it's a start."

I was horrified, "You didn't take more?"

Becky leapt to her feet, "They've got me over a barrel, haven't they? I'm in debt up to my ears, they can send me to prison - what am I supposed to do?" Her lips started to tremble and tears sprung to her eyes. Becky had always seemed so stoic and yet here, perhaps, was the real her; a frightened young woman, way over her head in something none of us seemed to be able to control.

I reached out to her and drew her into my arms. I don't know why I did it, but having experienced the pleasure of Destiny's hug it felt like the right thing to do. Besides, I was her father and that's what fathers do. I was about thirty years too late, but the instinct was there nevertheless. At first, she resisted the contact, but after a moment she relaxed and sobbed into my shoulder.

I soothed her as best I could, "There, there. I'm sure it will all be alright. There, there."

Becky sniffed, "You're rubbish at this."

"Sorry, I'm still finding my feet."

She stepped back and smiled as she wiped her eyes on the sleeve of her jacket.

"Are you alright?" I asked.

"I will be when this is all over."

"Well, we're getting closer. We have one more day to resolve this, I have faith."

"Whoop de do," Adam mumbled.

"It's such a shame Maggie hated children," Mother said, blowing her nose on a tissue.

I resumed my seat, "She didn't hate children; she illustrated children's books, she loved children."

"I always said you'd make a good father one day."

"We just didn't want any of our own."

"You mean, *she* didn't."

"Well, I couldn't very well produce them on my own, could I?"

"Aha, I knew it was her! I said to your father, she's too selfish to have kids. There'll be no grandchildren for us if that marriage lasts!"

"Mother, that's enough. Maggie was anything but selfish. She felt she wasn't suited to motherhood, and I wouldn't have a clue how to be a parent – just as you didn't! For once and for all, I never wanted children..."

There was a sniff in the darkness, "Oh, thanks a bunch," Becky said.

"I'm so sorry, Becky. I didn't mean now or *you*. This has been a lovely... surprise. *I'm* quite surprised. It all seems so natural, so normal. Well, it *is* normal, you are normal... I mean..."

Mother blew her nose again as she leant across to me, "I'd stop digging before the hole gets any bigger, if I were you."

I needed to find some order in the growing chaos and reached for the little notebook in my pocket, but found it empty. I took a steadying breath and raised my hand instead, counting each item off on my fingers, "Let's recap our progress so far;

1.Denis is not Ellis or Seven.

2. We know that Callum was not murdered by anyone.

3. We have Destiny on board, so we have someone else on our side."

I slipped from my seat and started to pace stiffly around the table, pausing behind Mother as she mumbled to herself whilst rubbing vigorously at her crystal, "For heaven's sake."

She opened her eyes and looked at me, "Do you need a paracetamol?"

"What? No, I do not."

"Hmm, I sensed some pain, that's all."

"I am perfectly fine. I'm trying to think, that's all. A new question is whether Seven could be a woman, something we had not previously thought about."

"I doubt it," Becky said.

"Why not? It's a very clever set up, it could easily be a woman," Mother said.

"Yes, but didn't Mrs A say she told a man where you were staying?"

"Yes, she did, but it might not be connected. On your list of seventeen local people named Ellis, how many were women?" I asked Adam.

He flicked a lank lock of hair out of his eyes and tapped away on his keyboard, "I got the list down to nine people, some were dead or had moved away. Of those, four are women," he said.

"Gosh, nearly half. I agree it seems unlikely, but we can't rule them out. With no other leads, I wonder if we should divide the list between us..."

Mother had started scrabbling around in her ever-present tote bag, "Wait, wait..."

Assuming some sort of mystic pebble or divining rod was about to appear, I ignored her, "It shouldn't take too long to track them down and..."

"Henderson, wait, look at this," she was waving a newspaper at me and began laying it out on the picnic table. "This is the local paper, The Bexhill and Battle Observer. I was reading it earlier while you were messing around with seashells. Here on the front page... look."

We all leaned forward, as Becky used the torch on her phone to illuminate a grainy photograph of a golf buggy with two men inside, under the headline, *Police Inspector Tees-off as Misconduct Probe Launched.*

"Do you see his name?" Mother said, pointing to the caption under the photograph.

"Inspector David Ellis," I read. "A crooked policeman called Ellis, bingo!"

"Let me see," Becky said, picking up the paper.

"Perhaps that's the link between you all," I said, with growing excitement. "Becky, you thought one of the policemen was suspicious of your insurance claim. Adam, have you had contact with the authorities in the past over your computer work?"

Adam threw a quick look at Becky, "Maybe."

"And Destiny revealed to me that she has a criminal record."

Becky started to fold up the newspaper, "Well, it says they're looking into possible embezzlement, links to organised crime and so on. It does sound possible."

I was too excited to stay still, so set off on another circuit of the trees, "It all makes sense. Who else would know what you've all done? It's the perfect operation, very clever..." I was halted in my excitement as my right foot disappeared into a rabbit hole and I tipped over in almost perfect slow motion.

Becky was the first to reach me, "Henderson, you are a liability, honestly, pull yourself together."

As I lay on the damp grass, nothing could dim my enthusiasm, "Bingo! It's him, I'm sure of it."

"You should get some rest, you're looking pale again," she whispered, as she crouched beside me.

"Yes, I do feel tired, it's been quite a day. I've booked myself into a B&B in the old town, I hope that's okay."

"Which one?"

"The House of Good Hope."

"Yes, that's nice. I suppose using a bucket is not really your thing, is it?"

"It was fun for a while, but I couldn't do it for ever," I said, but didn't move as I was rather enjoying the lay down. "Everything will be alright, Becky. I promise."

"You promise? I'm not sure you can do that."

"No, I think I can. I just have a feeling that things are about to change."

"Maybe you're psychic like your mother. Now clear off, get some rest. It looks like we have a golfing policeman to track down tomorrow."

# CHAPTER 14

Mother went down like the Titanic, slowly at first and then full steam ahead until she was face down on the turf. The golf ball that had ricocheted off her head rolled down the steep slope and, to my horror, Mother's limp body followed it. Before I could get to her, she had rolled right into a bunker.

Becky and I rushed from our hedgerow hiding place and across the green. We knelt and turned her over, brushing sand from her face.

"Mother? Do you recognise me?" I said, trying to sit her up.

She slowly opened her eyes, "It's either Howard or Clark Gable."

"Bloody hell," a panicked voice said from the edge of the bunker above us. "Is she alright? What were you doing on the fairway?"

I turned and looked up into the puce face of a pink-clad golfer, "Actually, we were looking for someone."

"Well, unless you're a member or have been signed in by one you shouldn't be here."

I lowered Mother back down onto the sand, "I have a

good mind to call the police. This is a defenceless old woman, knocked senseless by your ball."

"Alright, calm down. Let's have a look at her," he stepped past me and knelt beside Mother. "Well, she's still breathing."

"Let's give her a moment," I said, struggling out of the bunker and standing on the high ground, looking down at him. Despite a better night's sleep in a decent bed, I had woken with a strange feeling about today. I had no idea why, except perhaps, it was the last day I should be here before heading home for D-Day.

It had started well with the morning bringing glorious blue skies, a well-cooked breakfast and Becky collecting me in an actual car. It wasn't hers, she had 'borrowed' it from a garage customer for the day, in order to transport Mother and I on our quest for Ellis.

Adam had managed to gain access to the golf club's booking system and informed us that Inspector Ellis was booked in for a round at ten thirty. We had arrived early at the Highwoods Golf Club and made our way quietly from the car park through the woods and thickets surrounding the course, to a hiding place by the green of the second hole. Mother had grown increasingly impatient as ten thirty came and went, then eleven, and by half past she was constantly sticking her head out of the greenery to look for Ellis, until tragedy and a little white ball had struck.

I cleared my throat, "Ahem, perhaps you can help us?" and I beckoned for the golfer to join me on the crest of the sandpit. He seemed reluctant to leave Mother, but eventually brushed the sand from his pink trousers and came over.

"She's fine, just a bit of a shock that's all," he said, a sour look on his pudgy face. "If you think you are going to sue me or the club, you have another think coming, my friend."

I smiled, "I have no intention of any such thing, but I do need your help with something. We're looking for someone called Ellis. David Ellis. Do you know him?"

"Dave? Yes, I know him. I was supposed to be playing him today, but he dropped out, last minute. Damned annoying, but not really surprising."

"Why isn't it surprising?"

"He's gone to ground, I expect. He was in the papers yesterday, dodgy dealing going on - and from a policeman. Not on, not on at all."

I nodded sagely, "I agree, but innocent until proven guilty, surely?"

He stabbed the ground with his club, "That'll be up to the Men's Captain. Bringing the place into disrepute, photo in the paper under criminal headlines."

Anyone would think he was on the front of The Times, rather than the local rag, but I let that pass, "But what has he actually done, does anyone know?"

The golfer looked around checking we were alone and lowered his voice, "Rumour has it there were ladies involved," and he tapped the side of his nose slowly.

"Good grief, really? I'd heard it was drugs, car theft that sort of thing."

"Well, Geoff, who I play with on a Tuesday, said that

was more in the line of his partner in crime. He had a pal he went into the police with when they were young, he was the real trouble. Dave tried to distance himself from this chap, apparently, when the rumours started. Then his friend popped his clogs. Hit by a car; old fella thought the accelerator was the break – easily done. Anyway, things went quiet after that for a while, then all this stuff with the ladies surfaced. Bad show, it really is."

"I see, well, thank you… erm?"

"Clifford."

"You don't happen to know the name of Dave's friend, who died, do you, Clifford?"

"No idea. Why so many questions? What's it to do with you?"

"Well, I…"

"Steady on, are you one of those paparazzi fellows? Snooping around in bushes, trying to get dirt on a chap?"

I stepped back, "Not at all…"

"You swine," he had gone even redder in the face than when he first arrived. "You fellas are the lowest of the low in my book. I'm calling Dave Ellis now to tell him to watch out for you, poor chap."

"Poor chap? You wanted him drummed out of the club a minute ago!"

Clifford was now marching away towards the club house, punching roughly at his phone, "He's a club member and we stick together … especially against thugs like you. I shall have you removed… ah, Dave, is that you?" he shouted.

I hurried back to help Becky drag Mother out of the bunker and make a hasty retreat.

* * *

Half an hour later we were hidden away at a back table of Café Amato.

"How's your head, Mother?" I asked.

She sat opposite me with an icepack held to her forehead, "Not too bad. I've heard that sudden trauma can enhance psychic ability; you know, draw back the veil between this world and the next. I may be able to see more clearly now."

Becky laughed, "Well, you didn't see that golf ball coming, did you?" She turned to me, "So, do you think he's our man? Is Dave Ellis Seven?"

"I'm not sure. Clifford didn't think much of him, but that doesn't really mean anything. He said that he thought Ellis was accused of being a ladies' man, rather than anything really dodgy. It was his old friend who was into criminal stuff, apparently. I'm none the wiser, to be honest." I was beginning to feel tired and in need of a tablet. That nagging feeling that something untoward was about to happen was getting stronger and was hampering my ability to think straight.

"Three Welsh rarebits," Mrs A announced, as she delivered our lunch to us. "Your drinks are on their way," and she whistled her way back to the kitchen behind us.

"Cheese on toast," I said, with a sigh. "Food of the gods."

"There are seeds in this bread," Mother said, poking the

toast with her fork.

"It's wholegrain, Mother."

She started to peel off the cheese to get at it.

Mrs A returned with our drinks and set them in front of us, "What a morning you've had," she said. "How did all this happen?"

"We were at the golf course," I said. "Things got a bit out of hand."

"I should say they did. You want to speak to the head honcho, let him know what happened and strike a deal. You know what they say, where there's blame, there's a claim."

"Thank you, Mrs A, we'll definitely think about it," I said, and she disappeared behind the counter to serve a family burnt scarlet by the sun.

Becky leant forward and tapped my hand with a teaspoon, "She may have a point."

"I hardly think the golf course is going to listen to a complaint from us."

"No, listen, we're running out of time and we're both in danger now," she said, running her hands through her hair. "You need to get back to sort out your... you know, stuff. Why don't we just speak to the Head Honcho directly, like she said. Let's ask Seven to face us?"

Mother flicked a seed from her toast across the table and it pinged off the pepper pot, "Oops, sorry. How would we do that?"

"Henderson could agree to hand himself in."

I choked on a piece of mustard encrusted cheese, "Eh?

Hang on."

Becky pushed the food to the end of the table, "Listen, if we tell him that you've identified Callum, Destiny and Adam and you use his name, Ellis, then he might agree to meet to strike a deal. He'll see we're on to him."

"Maybe. And if it is Dave Ellis, he'll know how close we are after Clifford's phone call telling him we were looking for him this morning," I said, feeling a rush of adrenaline.

"Exactly. We'll tell him you have a dossier with all the information the police need to track him down, and if he does you any harm it'll automatically get sent to them," Becky's enthusiasm was obvious. "It's Friday tomorrow, you wanted this all sorted before then, didn't you? This way you can be home by the morning."

As I looked into Becky's grey eyes, everything fell into place. The truth was, I no longer needed D-Day or to rush home, the decision was already made.

"Actually, Becky, there is less of an urgency to be back – certainly not before Monday. I have decided to go ahead and to fight on. Whatever it takes, for however long it gives me."

Mother looked up from picking out her seeds, "How long what gives you?"

We ignored her, this moment was solely between me and Becky. I saw something change in her eyes, just a flicker, but I was beginning to know her well enough to register these things, "I thought you would be pleased?"

She blinked and looked away, "I am. Of course I am, if it means you have more time."

"Time for what?" Mother's voice was now insistent.

149

"What are you talking about? Howard? Rebecca?"

"It doesn't mean we shouldn't move swiftly on Seven," I said. "Text him now."

"No, I suppose not," Becky said, pulling out her phone.

I suddenly felt famished and pulled the Welsh Rarebit back in front of me, "If I'm going to face him later and the torment of the next few months, I'm going to do it on a full stomach."

"If someone doesn't tell me what is really going on here, I am going to throw this piece of toast at the next person who walks through that door!" Mother said, with predictable drama.

Becky shot out of her seat, "It's him! He's just messaged me."

My stomach lurched, "That was quick."

She whooped and sat down again, "I haven't even texted him yet. Yes! He says he wants to meet, just you and him. One to one."

"Good heavens," I said, my mouth suddenly dry. "We didn't even have to force him. He must know we're closing in. Does he say where?"

"The top of Galley Hill, tonight at midnight. He says come alone or there will be consequences. God, he's dramatic, isn't he?"

Mother laid her buttery hand on mine, "Howard, I know you're trying to help everyone, but I don't like it. Something's not right. He's been so secretive up to now, why would he suddenly want to meet you? I have a bad feeling."

"You and your feelings, Mother," I said, wiping the grease from my hand. "I have my own intuition and it says Seven knows he's facing a worthy adversary, that's all. We need to finish this. When I've seen who he is, he's lost. We can reveal his identity just as he can expose Becky's crime and that of the others. Stalemate."

"Well, it all sounds very heroic, but I hope you know what you're doing," she said. "Make sure you wear your suit, people always take a man more seriously in a suit."

"Good idea," I said. "I'll give it a quick spruce-up back at the B&B."

Becky beamed at me and leant across to give me a kiss on the cheek, "I appreciate everything you've done to help us. You're amazing... Dad."

If I had any reservations about facing Seven alone, at that moment they evaporated. I was ready.

# CHAPTER 15

From the window of my room at The House of Good Hope I had a pleasant view over the roofs of Bexhill old town, and got lost in my thoughts as the sun slowly brought Thursday to a close.

My world had transformed itself in the space of just three days. What I had thought would be a polite introduction to a young woman I had no real connection with, had turned into something much more significant. I had become her dad. As a result, here I was ready to undergo any medical treatment required for a few more weeks or months of my extraordinary new life – thrilling, chaotic and yet full of purpose. I just had to get through my meeting with Seven.

This would be the first time I would be a lone sleuth, no back-up from Becky or Mother, facing Seven with just my wits and a somewhat worse for wear Irish linen suit.

I dressed carefully, choosing a clean white shirt and strong red tie to go with the suit that I had spent some time trying to revive during the afternoon. It was certainly passable now. Becky was to pick me up at eleven fifteen, but I was ready far too early and paced the room feeling increasingly queasy.

Between visits to the toilet, I sat on the edge of the bed, too anxious to even think of supper, increasingly believing the whole thing was doomed to failure. Who was I to try and trick a hardened criminal? How could Howard Henderson, overweight, semi-depressed upholsterer, who hadn't even had the guts to face his own cancer treatment, stand up to the likes of Seven? It was foolish beyond belief.

I was ready to call the whole thing off when the chug of a vintage motorbike drifted through the faux leaded windows of the B&B. When I looked out, Becky waved at me from the end of the front garden. There she was, my daughter, who was relying on her long absent dad to finally be of use to her. Was I really about to let her down?

I stepped back and checked myself in the mirror. I chose not to look myself in the eye, afraid of the cowardice I might see. The truth was, if Maggie were here, she'd be the one climbing to the top of the hill to rescue everyone, not me. I'd be waiting at the bottom with a flask and the location of a good restaurant to have dinner afterwards.

I winced, was that my legacy? The back-up man, who stood a few steps behind when anything interesting happened. I squared my shoulders, "Not anymore," I said to my reflection. Looking at myself in the eye, I smiled, "The Seagull has landed."

The road up to Galley Hill was a long one, starting at the end of the promenade. Becky had decided to bring the bike as it was speedier than the car if a quick get-away was required, and she tucked it out of sight behind a large bin.

"This is as far as I can go without being obvious,"

she said, pulling me out of the sidecar, with practiced expertise. "It'll take you a few minutes to walk to the top, but I can be up there in a shot if you need me."

"I'm sure that won't be necessary," I said, hoping I sounded convincing. "We're only going to talk. Once he's fallen into the trap of revealing himself, it shouldn't take long to persuade him the game is up. I'll be back before you know it."

"Yes, I'm sure you will," she said, fiddling with the strap on her helmet. "Look, erm, Henderson... Dad. Can I ask you a question?"

"Of course, anything."

"If the treatment doesn't work, for the cancer-thing, or you don't go through with it, how long did they say you had to, you know, live?"

"Well, they weren't entirely sure, prostate cancer can move slowly, but they also found a shadow on my lung so the fear is that it's on the march elsewhere. I assume it's a question of months. They suggested if I was lucky, I might stretch it to a year."

"That long," she whispered.

I laughed, used to her humour by now, "I know it doesn't seem much, but a lot can happen in a short space of time. I've learnt that since coming to Bexhill."

"Look, maybe this isn't such a good idea. I mean you're not really..."

She was clearly nervous on my behalf, perhaps embarrassed that she had put me in this situation, "Becky, I appreciate your concern, but it really is time I did something useful with my life. Speaking of which, I'd like to ask you a question? And I don't want you to be embarrassed."

She removed her helmet and nodded, without looking directly at me, "Sure, what?"

"How bad is your financial situation?"

She sighed, "Not your problem. Don't worry about me."

"But it should be my problem, I think your mother sent me so you would have someone to worry about you. Perhaps I can help."

She looked at me, it was hard to see her face clearly, as there was little moonlight and the nearest street lamp wasn't working, "How?"

"Well, I was wondering if a loan would be of any use?"

She scrubbed her hands through her hair, "A loan?"

"I should have brought it up before, I'm sorry. We can sort something out, a payment scheme. You're working at the garage, once your debts are paid off, you'll be able to pay me back."

"And if you died before then?"

I took the handkerchief from my pocket and wiped my forehead where the helmet had caused me to sweat, "Gosh, I hadn't really thought of that."

"I didn't mean it to come out like that, but unless you have an awful lot of money to spare, I don't think you can help me."

"A lot? Oh dear, no, Becky, not really to spare. I'm not a poor man, but what I do have is spoken for – Mother, a few elderly aunts, Maggie's family - when I'm gone, that is."

Her laugh sounded hollow, "Of course, it is. They're

family after all." She kicked the gravel with her black boot, knelt down and began a fierce adjustment of something around the tyres.

I stood for a moment, too stunned to move. She was right; I had made provision in my detailed preparations to take care of my family and Maggie's, never once considering her within that group. How stupid! How hurtful for Becky, to suddenly have a father thrust upon her and realise she had been landed with one who was such an unfeeling idiot.

"Becky..."

"Don't worry about it," she said, her voice hard. "I'm fine, I've got some money coming my way."

"Do you? Excellent, well..."

"Just go and meet Seven."

"Yes, of course. I should be off or I'll be late," I turned and began to follow the road up the steep hill. First thing in the morning, I would contact Simon Moon and ask for an amendment to my will to include a gift for my daughter, for Becky. That was easy to fix.

Bexhill was a town that had very little night life and as I continued into the darkness, I knew that I was alone and the next person I was likely to meet would be Seven himself. I felt my bravado slip a little.

There was a light breeze coming off the sea to my right, which slowly died away as I plodded up the hill beside the edge of the cliff. As I reached the top I checked my watch, it was a couple of minutes before twelve. Bang on schedule, even allowing me a little time to catch my breath.

The moon was neatly tucked behind a thin bank of clouds, casting the softest of lights over the scene. I stood as close to the edge as I dare and watched the waves gently roll over the rocks far below. The sound of them washing the day away became hypnotic in the otherwise silent night. A seagull caught my eye, swinging through the pockets of air over the sea. Its presence was comforting and I felt a little braver.

I was enjoying the calmness that surrounded me when an itch began at the base of my neck – the Henderson Niggle. It told me that a big moment was upon me and I turned.

As I did so, two hands reached out of the darkness and thumped into my chest. They pushed hard and I was forced backwards, my feet stumbling unwillingly across the ground until there was no more grass, no more earth. As I fell, the moon broke from the cloud and lit Becky beautifully, her arms outstretched as she launched me into the void.

# CHAPTER 16

Falling is both thrilling and terrifying. Everything is beyond your control. Chaos in its purest form.

I remember flashes of the pink cliff as I rushed past it. Grey soil, tufts of green grasses, a white seagull floating in the air. I knew it would end with a rock at my back, but all I could think of was two pretty, grey eyes cold as steel.

The impact was like the moment on the very edge of sleep when you suddenly jolt awake, the shock taking your breath. It only lasted a second and then a light breeze blew across my fingers, up my hand to my wrist and on to my arm. Its coolness reached my cheek and trickled delicately across my eyes, forcing them to close.

With the soft air soothing me, I felt the weight that held me to the earth loosen and I was lifted from the rock. Weightlessness is an extraordinary thing, especially for someone of my proportions - joyful, warm, reassuring.

The breeze that surrounded me shifted tenderly as I moved from one thermal to another over the sea. I didn't need to open my eyes, I knew the sky was clear above me, the clouds gone and stars bright to guide me.

Gradually, a single sound, like the softest note held

on the flute, sent an energy through me and my arms reached out towards it. The waves below rolled against the note and drove me on making the need to rise more urgent. I was gaining pace, moving with greater speed away from the sea.

As my arms pulled me upwards, first one fist clenched then the other. The powerful calm that engulfed me started to fracture as I fought to slow down, to stay close to the earth. I wasn't ready to leave. I began to fight.

I twisted one way then the other, trying to free myself from the grip of the wind that was taking me away. I couldn't yet open my eyes, but I was able to speak, "No."

I spoke softly at first, then felt my voice grow in strength, "No. I'm not ready. I must go back. NO!"

My body lifted and turned so I was no longer on my back. I felt the air shift and instead of rising I began travelling forwards, my head leading the way. I had no idea how far I had to travel, but I kept repeating, "Take me back. She didn't mean it. Please, take me back."

My eyes opened and began to focus; I was high above the sea, the lights of the town mere pinpricks on the horizon. I knew I had to return and my arms opened wide, catching the cool air beneath them and I floated towards the land. Soon I could make out the streetlights along the seafront promenade, the warm glow of illuminated windows, even Bertha's flashing fish and chips sign.

I felt a presence to my right and turned to see the seagull gliding beside me, wings extended within reach of my fingers. I stretched towards it, but it kept its distance, focussing on the cliff face that appeared ahead of us. It moved in front of me, as if bringing me back, and

I followed.

We rose high above the cliff, circling once, twice. The sky had darkened again, clouds masking the moon, but I could make out a dark figure below me. The seagull turned its head slightly and our eyes met for a moment, then it adjusted the angle of its feathers and soared up and away, back out to sea. I looked down and slowly began to descend, until my feet were just above the ground. I seemed to hover for a fraction of a second, as if making sure this was what I wanted.

"Yes," I said, and touched down on the earth, a single white seagull feather falling silently beside me.

I wasn't sure how long I'd been gone, but I knew that everything had changed. I, Howard Henderson, was dead.

I knew for sure that I had died on the rock at the base of the cliff. How, then, was I standing on the top of Galley Hill again, staring at the back of my daughter as she looked down into the darkness, where I presumed my body still lay? I was... what? A ghost? A spirit? A shadow?

I looked down and saw my comfy shoes, my cream linen trousers, my jacket, my red tie, all still intact - not wet from the waves or torn from the rocks. In fact, my suit looked better than it had when I tried to revive it earlier that evening for one final wear. I touched my stomach, still there, out in front – sadly, no improvement on that score. Then I realised the background pain and tension that had been my constant companion prior to and, increasingly so after my diagnosis, had gone. No ache in my back, throbbing in my hips, even my bladder felt blessedly tranquil.

I wiggled my toes; I could feel them move but not make

any real contact with the ground beneath my feet. I took a tentative step forward and the grass was soft, almost spongy, as if I was barely putting any weight on it. It was a strange feeling, but not unnatural.

I changed my focus to Becky. It appeared that she hadn't moved, but now her arms hung loosely by her side. This could be a little awkward, I thought, as I took another step towards her.

"Becky," I said. My voice sounded normal, but had a slight echo to it - faint, like I was in an empty room or church. "Becky?" I tried again, this time louder.

She didn't respond, no shock or horror. Nothing.

I moved to stand beside her. It was still dark, but I could see her face quite clearly. She was staring down at where I had disappeared. There were no tears, no look of alarm, just a slight shiver. Perhaps she was in shock and it was all a terrible accident. She had rushed up the hill to tell me something, in her panic she had stumbled and pushed me over, saving herself at the last moment, but unable to save me.

Becky moved, pushing her hands deep into the pockets of her jeans and grinned. She actually grinned - a cold, contemptuous grin. Then she spoke, barely above a whisper, but the words were clear, "Goodbye, Daddy-dearest."

Next, she pulled out her pink kitty phone and typed a text, "Job done," she said and tapped send with a flourish.

"Becky, Becky," I said, as she turned away from the cliff and began to jog down the hill. I saw her tap on the phone again and place it to her ear, "Police and ambulance, please..." she said, as I watched her back disappear into the night. Soon I heard the familiar rumble of the motorbike, which faded away towards the town.

It had not been an accident. Becky had deliberately, knowingly pushed me. My own daughter. I felt my knees starting to give way (that hadn't changed then), but this was not the time for weakness. I forced myself to pace in a circle across the grass. I tried to make sense of the new reality, but it was all too much. My mind wouldn't settle on any one thought. It flitted from Becky, to the jolt as I hit the rock, the seagull, Becky's eyes, the sound as I hung in the air, the feeling of being pulled towards the stars, the memory of Becky's soft kiss on my cheek this afternoon, my hand in hers...

...Order. I needed to find some order in all of this. That was what I had been good at... *was still* good at. I sped up my pacing. I needed a list, lists were good. I thought of my little notebook, now laying at the bottom of the boating lake. My hand went instinctively to my trouser pocket, where it always sat and I froze as my fingers closed around its small, square shape. I could feel it - its weight and solidity. Relief washed over me and I released a long breath. I reached inside the pocket, but it was empty. Nothing. No notebook, no cotton handkerchief, not even a biscuit crumb which often lingered in the fold at the bottom. I looked down and could see its shape through the soft linen, but my pocket was empty. Then I understood; its comfort came from knowing it was with me, so it had been given to me – its presence only – to reassure me and give me some degree of resilience to navigate this new reality. Strangely, I did feel reassured.

I stood up tall and began a list, raising a finger:

*1. Am I dead?*

Yes, I should deal with that one first. I stepped to the spot Becky had just vacated, took a deep breath and looked over the edge. Far below on a large rock lay... me. My pale jacket spread out like wings, one leg tucked under the other, one arm hanging limply off the rock where the waves nudged it back and forth. I was surprised that I felt so calm, a steady strength seemed to have taken hold of me and I was able to process the information with rationality rather than the heat of emotion that I would normally expect.

Good, that's point one sorted - I was indeed dead and had travelled out of my body somehow. I was now back on earth in some other form having refused to go quietly into the night. This was incredible, there *was* an afterlife.

Clearly, I had unfinished business in Bexhill-On-Sea and was determined to see it through. I had no idea how, but I was certain that was why I was here.

The enormity of what was happening rolled across me and I walked to a bench, conveniently placed a little way back so people could enjoy the view. I sat. The wood no longer felt hard, but had a soft quality that cushioned my rear. I took deep breaths, but any chill in the night air failed to register in my throat or on my skin. It was all very strange, but equally fascinating.

Maggie's face came to mind. Where was she? Had she resisted too? Good grief, she would have fought tooth and nail not to be led anywhere she didn't want to go. I looked around, but appeared to be alone.

I settled back onto the bench, logic and structure making things easier to deal with. I held up another finger:

## 2. Why has my daughter just thrown me over a cliff?

This was more difficult. We had been getting on well, hadn't we? She'd said such nice things this afternoon and kissed me. She had even called me Dad. What could she possibly gain from my death? Bingo! Now we were getting somewhere, this was a better question. Why dispense with me when I was about to release her from her criminal responsibilities to Seven? Hang on, there's another good question.

One more finger joined the previous pair:

## 3. Where is Seven?

Becky and I had arrived here in time for our meeting, so now Seven was late. Had he been scared off by seeing me and Becky? Had he intended to come here at all? Bingo! Could he have forced Becky to get rid of me? Had he offered her some sort of incentive? Earlier, when we arrived, she told me that she had some money coming her way. Surely, she wouldn't have solved her debt problems by becoming an assassin?

I was getting nowhere; I just couldn't see Becky as a cold-blooded killer. I was her father, no daughter could do this, surely? I would have to do some more thinking, however, before I was able to continue, the shrill sound of sirens wound their way up the hill. I stood to see flashing blue lights heading along the seafront towards me.

I looked for somewhere to hide. I wasn't sure if I needed to conceal myself, Becky hadn't been aware of me after all, but I felt safer watching from afar. Until I got the hang of the rules of my new existence, I needed to err on the cautious, so I stepped behind the bench and into the bushes.

Soon, the top of the hill was alive with police and two tired looking paramedics, who all gathered at the cliff edge and looked down shaking their heads.

"Silly sod," the youngest of the three police officers said, getting a punch on the shoulder from his sergeant.

"Show some respect, Luke," he said. "You've no idea what he was going through to do something like this."

A female PC looked at him, "Shouldn't we keep an open mind, Sarge? Not assume he jumped, I mean?"

"Yes, yes, of course, officially, but this is a regular place for this sort of thing. Still, you're right, we need to do it by the book," the sergeant said. "Young Luke, tape off the area so no one thumps about in their wellies across any evidence. Claire, check out CCTV, but I'm pretty sure they haven't replaced the one at the foot of the hill yet or got around to putting a camera up here."

The paramedics were still looking down at me, "We'll have to go back down and walk along the beach," one said.

"Yeah, the tide's on its way out," said the other. "So, we should be alright."

The sergeant nodded wearily, "I'll come with you and contact the coast guard, just to be sure."

After reading so many crime novels, it was mesmerising to be in the centre of a real crime scene and the beginnings of an investigation - despite the small issue of the victim actually being me. I assumed Becky's call to 999 earlier had brought the emergency services, but she hadn't returned to explain what happened or her role in it. The chance of her innocence was becoming less and less likely by the minute.

PC's Claire and young Luke had concluded their tasks and were back at the top of the cliff, looking down at my body. I carefully came out of my hiding place and joined them, neither acknowledged my presence.

"I hope I don't get the short straw," Luke said.

Claire looked at him, "What short straw?"

"Telling the next of kin. I hate that bit."

Next of kin? Mother! Good grief, I didn't know what I could do, but I had to get to her.

# CHAPTER 17

I set off down the hill at speed, but halted after a few minutes as it struck me – I was not out of breath and nothing new ached. Perhaps I was free of all that now? Even so, it was going to take me an awfully long time to get anywhere if I had to travel on foot. It would probably take an hour to get to the Sunnyside Guest House from here, even in my new state. I began to walk more quickly and pictured the oak panelled hallway I was heading for, which Becky and I had entered hand in hand only a few days ago.

I'm not sure what made me do it, but as the image became clear in my mind I closed my eyes and took a large step forward. The next moment I found myself standing at the bottom of the polished stairs next to the chiffonier. No whoosh or sensation of travelling, I was just there in the guest house. There was clearly a lot more to discover about wherever or whoever I was, but that would have to wait.

I made my way up the wooden stairs of the guest house, with no creaks or groans under my weight this time. There were six rooms on the landing, but I knew that Mother was in the room I had occupied. I stood outside the door and knocked gently. Although I felt the solidity of the wood under my knuckles, there was no sound. I tried again. Nothing. This was going to be tricky.

Oh well, nothing ventured, nothing gained, I thought, as I took a step back and walked straight at the door. I was disappointed that instead of passing through I simply came to a sudden stop against it. No pain, no noise, just no entry.

How had this worked before? I had pictured the hallway and bingo! I tried to think of the room as I had last seen it. My clothes strewn across the bed, my bag in the corner by the wardrobe. Before I knew it, I had taken a large step and was inside the room. The bed was empty. I turned to the window and there was Mother, staring out at the moon which had shaken off its covering of clouds.

She looked tiny standing alone in her children's pyjamas, the only size that would fit her properly. The moon lit her white hair with an almost ethereal quality. I thought of the news that would soon shatter her life into a thousand pieces, and I sat quietly on the bed.

Was it my movement or a change in the air? I'll never know, but she turned and said my name, "Henderson?"

I leapt up, "Mother?"

Her cheeks were wet with tears, "You've gone, haven't you?"

"How can you know that?"

She hesitated, "I don't know."

"Hang on, can you hear me?"

She nodded, "Yes, just. You're very faint, don't mumble."

"How could you know?"

"I've no idea, but a little while ago I got a terrible pain, here," she touched her hand to her chest, just above her heart. "And I knew. I knew you weren't here anymore."

"I am so sorry."

"Are you really gone? I mean, not just in a coma somewhere? I saw a film once..."

"No, Mother, no."

"Was it him? Seven?"

"Ssshh," I said. "Can you hear that?"

"What?"

Through the partially open window came a distant roar that grew louder as it approached.

She frowned, "Is that...?"

"Becky! Mother, you need to listen to me. Don't ask questions, just run. Run!"

"Why would I run from Becky?"

"She was there, when I... you know. I don't fully understand it myself yet, but she's not what she seems."

"She's what? I can't hear you properly, Howard, you're mumbling again."

I listened to the motorbike engine die and go silent. Becky was right outside the front gate.

I moved closer, so that my mouth was beside her ear, "Mother, listen..."

"Oh, that's better."

"I think Becky is dangerous. It was her, she pushed me

off the cliff."

Mother staggered slightly, I reached out to catch her, but felt nothing and she righted herself with the help of the window sill. My breath caught in my throat as I understood what I had lost - the ability to touch another person and to be touched. It hadn't seemed important until recently. I had never been a fan of intimacy, but now it had gone it felt like the greatest loss.

There was no time to dwell on my change of circumstances, "Mother, are you alright?"

She spoke so quietly I could barely hear her, "No, I'm not alright. My only child tells me he's dead and that it was my granddaughter who killed him."

"I know it's a lot, but I need you to trust me. You need to get away from her and from here as fast as you can."

Mother rushed to the bed, putting on her heavy glasses and slipping her feet into her purple jelly sandals, "If she killed my son, then nothing on this earth... or the next, or wherever you are, is going to keep me away from her. I only want five minutes with her Howard..."

"No!" I said from behind her and she swung round. "Please, Mother, I have to keep you safe. I don't know a lot about what's happening to me, but I wasn't ready to go. I fought to come back for you and Destiny, Adam and... well, to find out about Becky. If she did this deliberately then she will pay for what she's done, but I need time to understand it. To work out why..."

Mother stopped, her hand on the door, "Where are you?" she asked.

"Where? I don't know yet, it's very hard to explain."

"No, I meant where in the room are you?"

"Oh, I'm standing at the end of the bed facing you."

She turned and looked directly at me, or where she believed me to be, "Howard, you are not a parent... well, not until very recently. You cannot understand what a parent would do for their child, or what she has taken from me."

"Mother, I think I was beginning to get a sense of it with Becky, which is why I won't condemn her out of hand. I need to understand her. I know you and I approach the world differently, but for now, please do this my way. I promise she won't get away with it."

She stood for a moment, staring across the room, more tears waiting to fall. Then she wiped her pyjama sleeve across her eyes, "Alright, Howard, let's find out the truth first. But I'm not running away from her. I am going to stand here and if she has come for me, then she has no idea of the fight she is about to have."

I had no more time to argue, as a soft knock came from the door, "Mother, pretend you know nothing, listen and see what she says. At the first sign of trouble, I want you to scream blue murder or blow one of your whistles that'll wake everyone in the street, never mind just this house."

Mother gave a small smile, "That's something I can definitely agree to." She turned to the door, "Who is it?" she asked.

"Oh, Mrs Henderson, I'm so sorry to disturb you. It's Mary. There is a young lady downstairs, Becky, she's a friend of your son. She says it's very urgent and it can't wait until the morning."

"It's alright, Mary, send her up."

"Of course... oh, you're here. Mrs Henderson says she will see you," we heard Mary's footsteps cross the landing and make their way down the stairs.

A moment later there was another knock at the door, "Sue? It's Becky, can I come in?"

Mother cleared her throat, "Ahem, yes, come in."

I watched the brass door handle turn slowly before the door swung open.

Becky was in her leather jacket, checked shirt and blue jeans just as I had seen her less than an hour ago, but I was looking at a different person. Colder, harder – untrustworthy. Was that there all the time, but I hadn't seen it?

"I know it's late, but I'm so worried," she said, as she stepped into the room.

"Has something happened? I've been waiting to hear from Howard about his meeting with Seven," Mother said, her voice sounding oddly cool.

Becky closed the door carefully behind her, and Mother began to sit on the edge of the bed, "Don't sit," I said and she shot back onto her feet.

"Why?" she gasped.

Becky turned, "What?"

"Why... why are you worried, Becky?" Mother said, awkwardly pulling at her pyjama top.

I got close to Mother, "Don't let her get between you and the door. You need to be near it so you can get out if you have to."

Mother nodded and started to move inch by inch towards the window, "Come and sit down, Becky. You look exhausted," she said, gesturing to the bed.

"Yes, I am," Becky said and moved further into the room. "It's Henderson..."

Mother continued to edge along the window towards the door, "I knew he shouldn't have gone up there."

Becky frowned, "Where are you going Sue? Come and sit by me, I need to talk to you." She sat and patted the mattress beside her.

"No, no, I prefer to stand. I get terrible cramp if I'm woken from a deep sleep."

"I thought you were waiting up to hear from Henderson?"

"Oh, yes, I was, but... what's going on, Becky?"

"So, I'd arranged to pick him up this evening to take him to Galley Hill. When I got to his B&B he wasn't there, the guy who runs it said he'd gone out earlier and hadn't come back."

I couldn't help but admire Becky's performance, she looked entirely genuine. Had it all been an act? I recalled our conversation as we had eaten our ice creams on the sea front,

"...I wanted to be an actress really. I was in all the school plays, but Mum wanted me to have a real job."

Perhaps Hazel should have let her follow her dream, I thought, she clearly has quite a talent.

"Why wasn't he there?" Mother asked, having reached the door by now.

"I don't know, I couldn't find him. I drove round for a while, but nothing. I texted Seven to see if they had him, but he said he was still planning to meet him at midnight. Eventually, I went back to the B&B and got the guy to open his room for me, which is where I found this," she pulled a crumbled piece of paper from her pocket.

My heart skipped a beat as she smoothed the sheet of paper between her palms. I stepped closer to her and she shivered. I paused, then took another step, she shivered again.

"Are you cold, dear?" Mother asked.

"It's me," I said. "When I get close to her, she shivers?"

Mother nodded and I heard her mutter, "Guilty conscience."

"Pardon?" Becky said.

"What a coincidence, Howard always wrote on that sort of yellow paper. He loved lists, ever since her was a child. Always scribbling away, it calmed him, you see. Funny little thing he was." She looked straight at Becky, "But he was very special."

Becky hesitated, "Was? Why do you say *was*?"

"Mother," I said. "Be careful." Becky looked ready to pounce, she was obviously on edge under her calm exterior.

"Well, when he was a child, not now. Now, he's not funny at all. So, what's that bit of paper then?"

Becky looked down at the sheet in her hand, "I think... I think it's a suicide note."

Mother started, her knees giving a judder as if they

were about to give way, and Becky moved swiftly to her side and took her arm – something I had been unable to do – but Mother shook her hand away, "I'm alright, don't fuss. Suicide? Not my Howard, never, never."

I wasn't sure if I was still able to blush, but I certainly felt heat rise through me as I saw what it was that Becky was holding.

"He's signed it, Sue. I think it's his writing too, but you'd know that better than me," she held the note out to Mother, who hesitated then took it from her.

I looked over her shoulder as she pushed her glasses up her nose and read it to confirm that it was indeed my writing – and it was. How had Becky got this? It should be screwed up in the waste paper basket next to my desk at home. Then things began to fall into place, *"You don't have an alarm? No CCTV?"* Becky had asked me.

Like a lamb to the slaughter, I had provided her with as much information as she needed, *"No, nothing."*

*"And I suppose you leave a key under a plant pot outside the door?"*

*"I'm not that foolish, Becky. It's behind a loose brick at the bottom of the door frame."*

Apparently, I am precisely that foolish! This wasn't a spur of the moment thing; this had been planned for some time. Carl & Slim ransacked my room to find my address and get access to the house, but why? No wonder she'd been worried when I mentioned the black dog of depression – she'd thought it was a real dog sitting guard in the house. But they couldn't have known I'd written this note before throwing it away. What were they really after?

Mother finished reading it and moved to lean against the door again, "I don't understand."

"I know, me neither... well, I have an idea, but I didn't know he was going to do this," Becky said, watching Mother carefully. "He didn't want you to know, Sue, he was protecting you, but he had cancer. Prostate cancer."

"No, Becky, no. I'm sorry, but that is not true. I'm his mother, I would have known that. He would have talked to me."

"He was a very private person."

Mother pointed her finger at Becky, "Don't tell me about my son. Don't you of all people tell me about him..." her voice choked and she couldn't go on.

Becky stepped towards her and narrowly missed brushing against me. She shivered and staggered slightly, "Damn, what was that?" she said.

Mother looked up, "What happened?"

"I felt... I don't know, like a little electric shock."

"We almost touched," I said into Mother's ear, and she smiled a sly little smile.

"This is a very old house, Becky, it's probably full of spirits, souls who have passed. You have to be ever so careful." She pulled herself up to her full tiny height and waved the letter at Becky, "Well, I don't believe it, this is not something he would ever do."

Becky let out a sigh, "I'm so glad you think that. I couldn't see it either, but knowing how ill he was I didn't know what to do, which is why I brought it to you."

Mother turned on her heels and went to her patchwork

tote bag that lay beside the bed, "We need to call the police. If he's gone missing, this is serious, not some silly game."

To my surprise, Becky agreed, "Good idea, I'm going to go back out looking for him. Let me know what they say," she crossed the room and opened the bedroom door.

"Wait," Mother said. "I don't have your phone number..." but Becky was already galloping down the stairs.

Mother ran to the door and shut it, turning the key in the lock. She then swung around, her face a picture of rage like I had never seen before, "Where are you? Howard, where are you?"

"I'm here, sitting on the end of the bed."

"Left or right side?"

"On the right."

She marched across the room and flung herself onto the bed beside me, then she slammed the yellow sheet of paper down between us, "This! Tell me about THIS. I am your mother and you are going to tell me exactly what you are playing at – dead or alive!"

# CHAPTER 18

This was a new version of Mother, or at least one I couldn't remember seeing before. Her eyes were pin sharp, she sat erect and alert on the bed, her short legs hanging down towards the floor.

"Well? I'm waiting, Howard. I know you think I'm some sort of idiot, but..."

"I don't think you're an idiot."

She scoffed, "Don't you dare lie to me. I've seen the way you look at me, the way you roll your eyes and try to apologise to other people on my behalf."

"I... I..."

"Yes, Howard?"

"I don't understand you, that's all. I don't understand how you can be so... colourful and extraordinary and believe all that tosh about the auras and the afterlife. It just doesn't make sense."

"Then how are you here, Howard? Or am I imagining all this?"

She had a point.

"I don't know, but until this happened it wasn't logical. None of it, the auras, the crystals it was all so silly. It made me uncomfortable."

"Howard, I was having fun. We're not in this world for long, so we might as well enjoy ourselves while we are."

"But I didn't want you to be fun. It was like you weren't afraid of the world and I really wanted to be like that too, but I didn't know where to start. All my school friends thought you were so funny, but I wanted you to be like their mums - being sensible and ironing things."

She sat quietly for a moment, "I could see you were a sensitive child and I was trying to help you let go a little. I wanted to show you how good it was to be a bit silly. I suppose I didn't do a very good job."

"You did your best. I'm not sure anyone would have got it right. I was odd, I heard Dad say that to you once. I didn't fit in and having a mother in rainbow skirts and Patagonian ponchos wasn't really what a teenager needed."

She smiled, "I suppose that could have been a bit embarrassing."

"Just a bit."

"Okay, but what about the cancer? Are you ill? I mean, were you ill?"

"About a month ago, I went to the doctor about my waterworks. Things weren't behaving as normal. They did lots of tests and said it could be cancer. They did more intimate and mortifying things and confirmed that it was advanced prostate cancer. They had also seen what looked like a shadow on my lung, so it was probable that it had spread."

"Howard," she said. "Hold my hand."

"I don't think I can, Mother."

She spoke so quietly that I had to lean in to hear her, "Please, just hold it. Tell me when you've done it, so I know."

Her hands were on her lap and I took my right hand and placed it over the top of both of hers. I could feel the shape of them and that they were solid, but I couldn't feel their warmth or the softness of her skin. I had not held my mother's hand for many, many years. Now I really wish I had.

"My hand is on top of yours."

She looked down, "Thank you. Go on."

"Well, I asked my doctor if I was going to die. She said all the right things, but it was clear that the answer was yes. With operations and then treatment I may have lasted up to nine months or a year. Without treatment, it was likely to be a lot shorter than that."

"Oh, Howard..."

"I was due to go into hospital on Monday, for it all to begin. But I wasn't sure I could face it. To go through all that fuss and the miserable days of recovery and still be dying – it just didn't seem worth it. So, I put my affairs in order and decided to make a decision today – Friday, as to whether I would go ahead with the treatment or let nature take its course."

She nodded again, "Did you want to go and be with Maggie?"

"I dreamed I'd join her at our picnic place on the South Downs; she'd be waiting for me there with some egg sandwiches. Isn't that stupid?"

"No, it's not stupid at all."

"Maybe, but I didn't believe in all that, did I? Then, on a very dark day, I thought that maybe I should just get on with it. That's when I tried writing the suicide note. I had no concrete plans to do it, but I thought if I could write something suitable, I might put it on the list as an option."

"Well, that was a bit stupid."

"I know, but I wasn't afraid of death itself, just the slow dying bit. Anyway, the note was so terrible I took suicide off the list. Maggie wouldn't have approved at all."

"I should think she wouldn't." She looked down at the note, "*To whom it may concern*," she read. "Honestly, Howard! *I've had a good life* – then you've crossed out *good* and written *nice*, then *pleasant*, then *interesting*, finally *unadventurous*."

"It's hard to know how to start these things. Anyway, I threw it away, I wasn't going to do it. It's funny, meeting Becky made me think there might be something worth living for and I should go ahead with the treatment. I was beginning to like my life a little more."

"I wish that had happened a long time ago, Howard," she took her right hand, lifted it and placed it palm down on top of her other one, effectively sandwiching mine in the middle. "Why on earth didn't you tell me?"

"I didn't tell anyone. Only Becky knew about it, oh and Simon Moon, my solicitor. I needed to work out what I was going to do, I'd written a list..."

"You and your lists! They are no replacement for talking to people, Howard, and human contact."

We lapsed into silence, perhaps both contemplating how my death had now robbed me of that contact forever.

Eventually, Mother spoke, "Have you seen Maggie, where you are now?"

"No, I haven't seen anyone else. It's all been a bit of a whirlwind, to be honest."

"You'll find her, if you want to. She'll be waiting for you, I'm sure of it."

"Thank you, Mother, that's a comforting thought. But before then, we have my murder to resolve and Seven to deal with. Ouch!"

"What is it?"

"I don't know, I felt a jolt, like someone shoved me from the side. Oof! There it is again," I got up and walked around the room. "It's very odd, it's like someone is touching me, but..."

"Your body," she said, hopping off the bed. "Your earthly body; I bet someone's found you. Where is it?"

"At the bottom of Galley Hill, on a rock."

Mother's head dropped, "Tell me what happened."

"I was standing on the edge waiting for Seven to arrive. Becky had driven me there."

"Lying cow."

"Mother, your language is getting worse."

"You haven't heard anything yet where that girl is concerned."

"Anyway, I was standing by the cliff, I turned and there was Becky. She pushed me, forcing me back and back until... until I went over the edge. I remember her eyes, they were hard and... cruel. Then she texted someone and said, *Job done*."

"Job done?"

"I assumed she'd messaged Seven. I wondered if he'd made her do it, or offered her money to silence me. But now I'm not so sure; that suicide note was at home in Brighton. Someone has been there and found it by chance, either her or Carl or Slim. But I can't work out what they were actually looking for."

Mother brightened up and rushed to her little suitcase on wheels, "Then that's where we start. We go to Brighton and see what they've done or what else they've taken. We have to follow the trail."

"I suppose so, it's as good a place to start as any. Oof!" There it was again, that strange feeling of being manhandled.

Mother was stuffing clothes and toiletries into her case as quickly as she could, "There'll be an early train. We need to get on with this, we don't want Becky to disappear before we can prove it was her."

Proof - why hadn't I thought of that? No one was going to take the word of a ghost or whatever I was, let alone his barmy, psychic mother. I checked my watch and it was now a little after one in the morning, "There aren't going to be any trains at this time of night. Besides, I expect the police will want to talk to you fairly soon. They've obviously reached my body and once they know it's me, they'll track you down."

She stopped what she was doing, "Yes, I suppose so."

"Why don't you try and get some sleep? Nothing much can happen until the morning. Becky's not going anywhere yet, she thinks she's set it all up nicely to look like I jumped on my own."

"She may be evil, but she's not stupid. Mind you, she'll have left clues and made some mistakes, they all do, and we just have to find them."

"Yes, but not now, Mother. Lay down and rest. It's going to be quite a day for you tomorrow."

"Maybe just for an hour or so, to give my feet a break," she said, as she sunk on to the bed. "You won't go away, will you, Howard? You'll stay here, won't you?"

"Of course," I said. "I'll just sit on the window sill and watch the moon. You sleep though."

"Fat chance," Mother said, with a sniff.

I spent the next few hours watching the moon and the stars. It was as if I had never really seen them before. The stars no longer looked like dots of light, but had each taken on their own shape and identity – as if they had suddenly come into focus. Even the moon seemed brighter and closer than before, like I was getting to know them all properly.

At exactly seven o'clock Mother's phone rang and she came to life scrabbling amongst the disturbed bedding to find it, "Where is it? Ah, here. Hello... Yes, this is Mrs Henderson... Oh, yes, hello... No, I'm not at home," she leant back against the pillows, then looked around the room, presumably trying to find me.

"I'm by the window," I said.

She pointed at the phone and mouthed towards me,

*"It's them. The police."*

"I'm in Bexhill on holiday with my son.... No, he's not with me at the moment. What is this all about? Do you have something to tell me?... I'd rather you just told me now... Yes, please...You've found what?" suddenly the room went very still and Mother seemed to shrink a little. Her voice became a croak, "Howard? Are you sure?" She nodded as she listened, "Yes, yes. Sunnyside Guest House. Thank you, I'll be waiting." She let the phone fall to her lap and started to weep.

"Mother?"

She sniffed quietly, "They've found you. I have to identify the body... your body. I don't think I can."

"Why? You know I'm gone, it's just a body now."

She spoke fiercely, "It's not just a body. It's *your* body. I created it. I gave it to you. No one has a right to... to..."

"It's alright, Mother, I'm here beside you."

"But when I see it, when I see you – you won't be there anymore. It'll be real. I'll know that I will never see you again."

"I'll still be here, Mother. Still with you."

She straightened her back, "Yes, you will won't you."

The sound of a car drawing up in the road outside came through the window, "I think the police are here."

She stood, "I'd better change. You'd be embarrassed if I went to identify your body in koala bear pyjamas, wouldn't you?"

"Yes, I would. Shall I come with you?"

She shook her head, "No, thank you. I'll do this alone,

no point you being there... it would just be confusing."

"Yes, of course. I'll be waiting for you when you get back."

"Are you sure?"

"Yes, Mother, I don't know how, but I know I'll be here."

"Good, that's alright then," she took a bright pink dress out of the wardrobe and threw it on the bed, the yellow suicide note fluttering away onto the floor.

"What are you going to do with that?" I asked. "Becky obviously wants you to give it to the police."

She picked it up and started tearing it into thin strips, "Over my dead body."

# CHAPTER 19

The morning train was depressing. Numb looking people, hunched over newspapers or their phones. Others shut away, their eyes closed and the sunny morning silenced by earphones. None of them seemed the slightest bit bothered that a lady with raggedy white hair, an enormous pink pinafore and purple glitter jelly sandals chatted to herself all the way to Brighton. In reality, Mother was filling me in on her interview with the police after a rough time at the mortuary.

"It just seemed to complicate things," she said on her decision not to mention Becky or Seven. "Plus, I don't want them disappearing if the police knock on their doors. We can tell the police everything once we've solved it all."

"That all sounds very sensible."

"Mind you, I'm taking a flask with me next time, their tea is filthy stuff. They asked me whether you'd been depressed or under pressure lately."

"Oh dear, what did you say?"

"I told Claire – very bright girl, she'll go a long way. I told her that you were always as sunny as a sunbeam, so there was no chance you'd have flung yourself off that cliff."

"Why on earth did you say that?"

"Apparently, they got an anonymous call from someone who had seen a fat man in a white suit standing on the edge of the cliff looking suicidal. I wanted them out looking for your killer, not fussing about whether you did it yourself."

I bristled, "My suit is cream not white and I don't know who would describe me as... ah... that must have been Becky. I heard her make a call and ask for the police and ambulance as she was leaving Galley Hill."

"Well, I told them there was no chance you'd have jumped. You couldn't even handle five minutes on a trampoline in Bournemouth."

I had only been seven, but I couldn't fault her logic.

"And the mortuary? Erm, identifying the... my body?"

"I don't want to talk about it."

"But..."

"No, Howard, you're here with me now. Not on some cold slab, looking..." she shivered and rubbed her eyes behind her glasses.

"Alright, I understand. Listen, I've been thinking about Becky and Seven and I'm convinced it's all some sort of plot designed to entrap me. I don't know why or how many of them are involved, but we need to find out the truth and quickly. I don't know how long I'm going to be here for."

She sat up straight, "Don't say that, Howard. But you're

right, that young woman is not getting the better of the Hendersons. This bloody grief can wait until she and the whole damn lot of them are behind bars."

My house was a short walk from Brighton train station, but I insisted Mother had some breakfast first. She wasn't keen, but she bought a hot chocolate with cream and marshmallows to drink as we walked. It must have put enough sugar inside her to power a small army, and she looked a lot brighter.

Maggie and I had converted an old corner shop on the end of a terrace of red brick houses. The shop became my workshop and her studio, and the upstairs we updated and turned into a large, comfy flat.

We went round to the rear of the house and Mother drew a brown envelope out of her patchwork tote bag, "Look at that," she said. "You'd have thought in a person's time of grief they'd find something nicer to put all your bits and bobs in, wouldn't you? A nice gift bag or something."

The plain brown paper with my name scribbled in biro at the top was a stark reminder that none of the items listed actually belonged to me anymore. My keys, wallet and some change, the pink kitty phone, my own phone, my cotton hanky and wedding ring all belonged to Mother now. I felt in the pockets of my suit, but they were empty, as was my hand where Maggie's ring had sat for so long. When I looked closely, I could still see a faint impression of where it had been.

I brought us back to business, "Shall we go inside?"

"Yes, which key is it?"

"Hang on, check that bottom brick beside the door, on

the left. Is there a key behind it?"

She leant down and wiggled the brick, "This one?"

"Yes, it should come out, we used to hide the spare there."

She worked the brick free, "No, nothing here, it's gone."

"That's annoying, I'll have to get the locks changed."

Mother put the brick back and stood up, "I'd like to see you try."

"Why? Oh, yes, I see. I'm still not quite into the swing of this new... situation."

"Howard, it isn't locked," she said, the door swinging open easily as she tried the handle.

"Good grief, they could be here now," I said, stepping back.

"Do you think? Well, go and have a look."

"We need to be careful."

"I do, but you'll be fine, remember?"

"Yes, yes, of course. Wait round the corner, out of sight. I'll call if the coast is clear."

I cautiously stepped inside my house, keeping close to the wall. Heavens knows why, as I could have skipped around singing Handel's Messiah and an intruder would still have thought they were alone.

I waited for a moment in the small hallway and listened. Silence, except for the usual ticking of the clock on the landing upstairs. It was strange to be back; being there, but also not being there. Everything seemed familiar and yet something was missing. I inhaled deeply, but there was nothing. No scent of polish from my workshop, ink and fixative from Maggie's adjacent studio. No smells of home anymore.

"Howard?" Mother called from outside, breaking my thoughts.

"Yes, just a minute. I'll check things."

I stepped through to my workshop directly in front of me, it was empty. An old Chesterfield sofa waited in vain for my attention, swatches of potential fabrics laying over its back. Maggie was the arbiter of colour and design when it came to the cloth I used. Since she had gone I'd struggled to match her eye or taste, so things took far longer than before. I could see her so clearly; cheerfully throwing fabric samples across the backs of chairs and then discarding them on the floor if they didn't meet favour. I would scrabble around her feet picking them up and dusting them off, as she tossed more aside. I chuckled.

She operated in much the same way in her studio, through a small archway from the workshop. When she was working on illustrations for a new book, paper would fly from her desk onto the floor, furniture and occasionally the light fittings during a particularly tempestuous session. I hadn't understood how she could work in such chaos, and in the early days I had tried to tidy up at the end of each day – but the tension grew too great. She insisted that the torn or screwed up papers were still in play, she might go back to them or reuse them, so they had to be left where they fell. She claimed to know exactly where each one was – I had my doubts, but it was easier not to argue. I always felt it was easier not to argue. Eventually we reached an agreement; I would be allowed in once a month to bring some order back to the studio, return the inks and paints to their rightful places and put the discarded papers in a box. It would only be emptied when the book she was working on was finished and in print.

I don't know how long I stood in the doorway to Maggie's studio. I hadn't felt able to go inside since she went – since I had found her on the floor, lying amongst a bed of crumpled papers. I had left it exactly as it had been on that awful day. The discarded drawings – trampled flat by the ambulance people - gathering dust, waiting, just in case they were still in play.

I took a step over the threshold. It was just a room. A chaotic, creative room, full of Maggie's work and colours; but she wasn't there. I laid my hand gently on the shape of my little notebook, feeling its comfort through the linen. She was gone, but now I was on my way to find her. I hoped I would find her. I gave the book a squeeze... no, I knew I would find her.

I stepped back into my own workshop, looking at the racks of tools as I passed, their wooden handles worn smooth by my hands. New hands would warm them in due course and I smiled. I had left instructions that all my tools should go to Maggie's niece, who had been fascinated by them and spent hours with me learning the use of each one. All the art materials would go to her nephew who, even at the tender age of six, was apparently showing signs of what Maggie had called a 'brilliantly disruptive Avant-garde bent' - whatever that meant.

I moved back to the hallway and crept slowly upstairs. I checked the kitchen, the bedrooms and living room, but I was alone. Finally, I tiptoed into the cubby hole we called the office and stood by my desk, with six neatly aligned manilla folders on its polished oak surface. Next to them lay the yellow legal pad, with my hand written To Do List.

I winced at the starkness of the list:

1. Go to Bexhill and meet daughter.

2. Decide on treatment & death later or no treatment & death soon.

3. Cancel newspapers.

4. Defrost freezer.

I couldn't imagine writing that list now, after everything that had happened in the last few days. It had been quite a week.

I leant forward to slide the pad into the bin, but although I could feel its solidity, my hand slipped across the surface. I sighed and called down the stairs, "Mother! It's all clear, you can come up."

A couple of minutes later she appeared at the top of the stairs, "It looks like they've tidied up rather than burgled the place. It's immaculate."

"That's how I left it, Mother."

"Oh, I see, well it's very impressive, Howard. Goodness knows what you must have thought of my house - actually don't answer that, I can guess. Oh, by the way, Mr Crawford says it was your brothers who broke in."

"Mr who? My brothers? What are you talking about?"

"I've just been chatting to your neighbour, Mr Crawford. He said that your brothers came to do some DIY earlier in the week – or that's what they told him. It sounds like little and large, he said one of them was a great big lump."

"Carl and Slim told Mary at the guest house they were my brothers too. Lucky Mr Crawford's very cautious with strangers in the street, he runs the Neighbourhood Watch."

"Well, he wants sacking, doesn't he? Letting those two come in and ransack the place."

"They haven't ransacked it, you just said it was immaculate. Anyway, sit here at the desk."

"What's all this?" Mother said, sitting in the office chair and looking at the folders.

"I was putting my affairs in order. I didn't know how long I had left, so I wanted to make sure things were straightforward for my executors. After Maggie's death it was a nightmare, so I wasn't going to leave things in a tangle for the solicitors or for you."

Mother sat very still with her hand on the folder labelled Funeral, "Is this for you?"

"Yes, it's all laid out. Who the funeral directors are, suggestions for music..."

"Stop," she said. "I don't want to know. We can deal with that later."

"Yes, of course. I need you to open the other folders, please, so I can see what's inside."

We started with Finance. I had left the papers aligned perfectly, no creased edges or pages upside down. Carl and Slim had been relatively careful, but I could tell that they'd looked through it all.

Mother picked up the top page, which was a printed

summary of my financial assets, and whistled softly, "Have you put the decimal point in the wrong place in this total?"

"Erm, no. That's how much I was worth as of last Sunday."

"But Howard, that's getting on for a million pounds," she spun in the chair to face me, but realised she didn't know where my face was. "Oh, blow, where are you?"

"Just over your right shoulder."

She did another full circle in the chair and stopped in front of me, "Howard, you never told me you were rich."

"I didn't really know I had quite this much until I added it all up. Maggie inherited quite a bit when her parents died, add to that almost every child in the country owning books she'd illustrated – it brings it to a decent amount. Then, of course, I worked with some well-paying clients, we invested in property and we didn't have children or expensive tastes, so it all added up, I suppose."

"Well, someone will be rich when they inherit all of this," she said, swivelling back to the desk.

"Yes, you are," I said, simply.

It took a moment for it to sink in, then she gasped, "Me? No, Howard, you mustn't leave it to me."

"There are gifts to friends and Auntie Sal and Auntie Bev, Maggie's Godchildren and niece and nephew, obviously, but the remainder of the estate goes to my next of kin. That's you."

She took her glasses off and started to clean them on the hem of her pink dress, sniffling quietly, "But I didn't think you liked me."

"Of course I like you. You're often very, very annoying, but you are still my mother and as I won't be there to see you through your old age, this will have to do."

"Stop it, Howard," she said, firmly perching the glasses back on her nose. "I don't want to think about that."

"Wait," I said, stepping closer to the table. "Open the folder labelled Legal. I wonder..."

She pulled the fourth folder towards her and opened it, "What am I looking for?"

I could already see what was missing. It should have been on the top, but instead I was looking at the deeds for the house.

"Howard? Are you still here?"

"Yes, sorry, Mother. Go through the pile, I need to see if my will is still there."

"Oh, my goodness, your will?" she said, as she rifled through the papers. There was nothing.

"We need to check the other files, quickly."

"Alright, hold your horses."

It didn't take long to establish that the will was the only thing that was missing. I moved away from the desk and looked out of the window, "It's all about the money."

"How do you work that out?"

"Whoever came here would have seen how much I was worth and who would inherit it. I'd laid it all out as simply as possible for them. Becky kept bringing up her money problems, the debt, the trouble it had got her in to, how the bank was going to stop her overdraft and so on. I bet she's not in debt at all. It was all to make me think she needed money – my money."

"She was probably hoping you'd just give her some to help her out or maybe a slice of the inheritance, as she was your daughter."

"Yes, come to think of it, last night she was a bit strange before I went up Galley Hill. She nearly changed her mind about me meeting Seven. Then after I'd offered her a repayable loan and told her that my estate would go to other people, she more or less ordered me up the hill. Was that my mistake? If I'd thought to give her some money as a gift or included her in my will, would she have killed me?"

"Howard, this is not your fault. Anyway, you haven't changed your will, so she's done it all for nothing. She won't get a penny from me, granddaughter or no granddaughter."

"Don't you see? I haven't changed it, but it's gone, so, *they* could have changed it."

"Who's they?"

"Becky, Seven, Carl, Slim, any of them."

"I hope you're not telling me that's the only copy, Howard? You of all people should know..."

"That's a good point, my solicitor has another copy."

"Well, we'll make sure he knows the one he's got is the proper one."

"Yes, it's with Simon Moon, Old Mr Moon's son. Do you remember him?"

"I remember his father, he dealt with everything when your father died. His aura was violet, very spiritual and wise – Old Mr Moon, not your father."

I was impatient to get going, "Come on, we need to get back to Bexhill and see Simon, make sure he has the other copy and warn him that a fake will might surface before too long."

We hurried out of the house, Mother locking the door with my key.

"I was thinking," she puffed, as we walked back up the hill to the station. "I must have a proper psychic gift, or how else am I talking to you? I wondered if I might try it out and see if anything comes to me about the people on the train. You know, see if I can reach anyone for them who's passed – like a proper medium or an intermediary. Or is it, intermedium? What do you think?"

I knew that she needed my support, but I wasn't prepared to listen to her try and read people's minds all the way back to Bexhill, "I'll probably travel under my own steam. I know what Simon's office looks like, I was in it on Tuesday, so with any luck I can picture it and go straight there."

"Is that how it works?"

"Well, it got me to you at the guest house last night. I'm going to give it a try, so if I go quiet, I'll meet you there."

"Alright, if you think that's best. Howard? Howard..."

But I was already standing in Simon's smart, beige solicitor's office, rather pleased that I was getting the hang of being dead... or at least the transportation part of it.

Simon was sitting at his desk, his puffy face looking strained as he held the phone tight to his ear, "Please do not shout at me... I am perfectly capable of dealing with it... Goodbye, Becky," and he slammed the receiver down.

# CHAPTER 20

I watched Simon stare for a long time at the phone he had just abused, but felt awkward eavesdropping like the invisible man, so sat in one of the client's chairs opposite him – the very chair I had sat in on Tuesday morning.

He sat back in his large leather chair and let out a long slow breath, "Marge, coffee," he shouted.

"And the magic word is?" came the reply through the door behind me.

"Please," he said in a more appeasing tone, before flinging two fingers in the air at the unseen Marge.

While he waited for his coffee, he picked up a piece of paper and proceeded to examine it in minute detail, bringing it close to his nose then moving it away at arm's length. His coffee arrived, delivered by a grey-haired woman in a home-knit sweater. He slipped the paper into a brown envelope.

"Thank you, Marge."

"You are welcome, Simon," she said, halting beside me at the edge of the desk. "Did I hear phone slamming again, Simon?"

He swallowed hard, "No."

"In the twenty-two years I worked for your father he never once slammed the phone. In the twenty-two months I have worked for you I have heard nothing but that phone being banged about."

"I'm sorry, it won't happen again," he said, looking at his fingers and their well bitten nails, as if he'd been caught with them in the biscuit tin.

Marge silently left the room, closing the door with a disapproving click.

Simon sipped his coffee then prowled the room until Marge returned to announce that his next client had arrived. It felt inappropriate to remain in the room while he met with them, and I certainly didn't fancy anyone sitting on my lap throughout the meeting. So, I spent the next hour or so in the company of Marge, who was clearly a meticulous worker, her desk neat as a pin. Her only vice seemed to be a discrete bag of wine gums hidden in the bottom drawer of her desk, which she dipped into every few minutes.

Eventually, soon after Simon's client had left, Mother arrived in a flurry of pink pinafore, her patchwork tote bag swinging across her shoulder, "Hello," she puffed to Marge. "I need to speak to Mr Moon, please."

"Do you have an appointment?" Marge said, as she scanned her from head to toe.

"No, but I need to see him. It's about my son, Howard Henderson. It's urgent. Ever so."

"I see, I can make you an appointment for next Tuesday," Marge said, consulting her calendar.

"No, it has to be today," Mother said. "I'll wait." She backed away from the desk and plonked herself down on one of the padded chairs, not taking her gaze from Marge's face or losing the smile from her own.

"He is very busy."

"We are all busy, my dear. Life is busy. Death is busy – believe me, far busier than you could even imagine. Let alone inconvenient. What with identifying the body, sorting out the paperwork - folders and folders of it. I had to do it for my husband. Mr Moon... Old Mr Moon that is, he was very helpful..."

"Please, please," Marge said, her face pinched at Mother's seemingly never-ending monologue. "I'll see if he is available. What did you say it was regarding?"

"The death of my son, Howard Henderson. I'm Mrs Henderson, his mother."

"Just one moment."

Mother watched Marge close the door behind her as she went to speak to Simon, "Howard? Are you here?" she whispered.

"Yes," I said, from the seat next to her.

"Oh, don't creep up on my like that."

"I wasn't creeping anywhere, I just happened to be sitting next to you. Now, listen, when I got here Simon was on the phone to someone called Becky. If it's our Becky then he's mixed up in this somehow, so you need to be cautious. If she were to find out you know what she did to me you'll be in serious danger. So, play it innocent, just ask to see my will."

"Yes, yes, leave it to me. I can handle young Simon

Moon," Mother said, as Marge silently returned to the room. "Has he still got piggy little eyes, a bit too close together..."

"Simon will see you now, Mrs Henderson," Marge announced, as she held the door open.

"Oh, lovely," Mother said, crossing the room and passing Marge. "You should never wear lilac, love, not with your aura."

"Mrs Henderson, what an unexpected pleasure," Simon said, with a toothy smile that didn't travel as high as his piggy little eyes. "What's this Marge said about Howard?"

She shook his hand briefly, "He's dead."

I watched Simon carefully, he didn't do a bad job at looking surprised, "I am so sorry to hear that. I only saw him this week, what a shock. Please, please sit down."

Mother perched on the edge of the client chair that I had used earlier and Simon went back behind his desk, "I knew that he was very unwell," he said. "But I understood it was a question of months not days."

"Yes, well, he fell off a cliff. But the reason I'm here..."

"Fell off a cliff?" Simon said, this time the shock seemed wholly real.

"Yes, well, I say fell. Pushed, fell - no one's sure yet."

Simon's mouth opened and closed like a puppet without a voice.

"Are you all right, Simon?"

"Yes, yes, it's just that I thought he..." Simon stopped himself and straightened his tie, sitting up straight in his chair.

I put my mouth close to Mother's ear, "He's definitely guilty of something."

I appeared to have surprised her again, "Don't do that," she hissed, jumping to her feet.

Simon stood up too, "What...? Are you alright?" he said.

"Me? I'm fine, just... just..." she searched for the right words, then smiled up at Simon, "I hear voices, I'm psychic you see. Probably someone from the other side wanting to get some advice from you. Sorry about that," and she lowered herself carefully back on to her chair.

He stared at her for a moment, cleared his throat and glanced nervously round the room as he sat back down, "I am very sorry for your loss, Mrs Henderson. Howard was a fine man. Obviously, I would be happy to help in any way I can."

"Oh, that's good," Mother said, sitting forward. "I'll take a look at his will, please."

Simon's hand moved a fraction across the desk, until his fingers lay on the edge of the brown envelope he had placed there earlier, "His will?"

"Yes, please. He told me you have a copy."

"Yes, that's right. I assisted him in putting everything in order when he got his diagnosis."

"I brought the will in on Tuesday," I said to Mother, from a short distance away this time.

"Tuesday, wasn't it, he brought his will in to you?" she asked innocently.

"Oh, you know about that will, do you?"

"Yes, we were very close. He told me everything."

I noticed the ends of Simon's fingers turn white with the pressure he was using to hold the envelope down on the desk, "Do you have a copy of that will, by any chance?"

Mother nodded, "Yes, well, no, he had one at his house..."

"Has," I corrected.

"I mean, *has* a copy at home, I believe, and you have one here, don't you?"

"Yes, that's correct. I shall need to check it, of course. You see, only the executors appointed in the will are entitled to read it before probate is granted. Why don't you come back next Monday or Tuesday? It's so soon after his death, you must still be..."

As quick as a flash Mother stabbed a finger at him, "How do you know it's soon after his death? Eh? I didn't tell you when he died."

"I... you... he was here yesterday, so it can only have happened last night or this morning," he stammered, sweat starting to trickle down his temples.

"He told me he brought the will in on Tuesday, not yesterday," she said, with another thrust of the digit.

Simon seemed to be vibrating with tension now, and his chair had started to rattle, "Yes, he did... on, erm, Tuesday. But he brought in a new will yesterday, he had revised it in light of..." he stopped and I noticed his eyes flick to the phone.

"In light of what?" Mother said, keeping up the pressure.

"In light of him... finding his daughter. I trust you know about Rebecca?"

"I know an awful lot about Rebecca," she tutted. "So, there's a new will? What does it say?"

"As I mentioned, until probate I can only reveal the contents to the executors."

"He's the executor," I said, frustration starting to make me pace the office.

"Isn't that you?" Mother said. "The executioner?"

"Executor," Simon corrected.

"Whatever you say. Look, Simon, I'm not asking you to write me a cheque for my share. All I want to know is that you have his will and what's in it. Surely you can do that for a grieving mother?"

I didn't think she looked particularly grieving at that point, so sharp was the glare she was giving Simon I almost felt sorry for him. This new fierce version of my mother was impressive and it was stirring memories. A time in the playground at primary school. A teacher backed up against a wall, his face pale. Mother, at least a foot shorter than him, shouting that her son would not do country dancing in his underpants if he didn't want to. I remember feeling pride. Gosh, I'd forgotten all that.

Simon's fingers drumming on the desk brought me back to the present, "It's a little tricky, Mrs Henderson."

"No, it's not Simon," Mother said, with a venomous gentleness. "What is tricky is explaining to all of your clients why this mad little woman is sitting in on all your meetings for the rest of the week, because she refuses to move until she sees that will," she shifted back in her chair and hugged her tote bag to her chest, her jaw clenched and eyes closed. She started to hum. I couldn't quite make out the tune, but it sounded a bit like All Things Bright and Beautiful.

Simon sat frozen in his chair, staring at her. It was a standoff. Not a very long one, though, as he lasted all of about forty seconds before he broke, "Alright, Mrs Henderson. Mrs Henderson?"

She opened one eye.

"I will give you the broad outlines of the will, but nothing is confirmed until probate has been completed, you understand."

She opened the other eye and nodded.

He sighed and drew the envelope across the table until it was in front of him. Slowly and with shaking hands he opened it, and pulled out the single sheet of paper he had been examining so closely earlier. I moved behind him so I could see it. It was printed on pale blue watermarked paper – the paper I used at home.

"You understand that your son produced his own will, so it may not have quite the legal finesse of one that we would draw up. However, it is legally binding."

Mother nodded, still sitting like a Chinese Empress, inscrutable and unmoveable.

Simon cleared his throat, "In essence, it is a simple document. Funeral expenses and any outstanding debts are to be paid from the estate, although Howard led me to believe that both were taken care of. There are a series of small gifts to family members, including yourself."

"Only fifty pounds," I said, reading over his shoulder.

"Ssshh," Mother said. "Go on, Simon."

Simon looked confused.

"Carry on, that shush wasn't for you."

"Oh, right, I see," he said, with a glance around the room. "Well, after these gifts the remainder of his estate will go to..."

We read the name at the same moment, "... Rebecca Richardson, his daughter."

I was not prone to anger, but as I saw Becky's betrayal in black and white a fire rose from my toes and rushed through me. With a yell I lashed out at the desk phone and it flew across the room.

We all gasped. I couldn't believe it. The anger had taken my hand through whatever barrier separated me from my old world, and I had felt the phone properly as I had struck it.

Simon was standing, his chair spinning on its own behind him.

After the initial shock, Mother rapidly returned to her calm state. She got up from her seat, picked up the phone and returned it delicately to the corner of the desk. Placing the receiver back on the cradle, she sat back down and shook her head at Simon, "You've got some shocking draughts in here, Simon. Now, where is the old will?"

"What? But how...?"

"Focus please, Simon. Time is money in your business, isn't it? Let's have you sitting down, shall we?"

He sat.

"Very good. Now, do you still have the will he gave you on Tuesday?"

Simon stared at the phone, but answered her question, "No, I destroyed it."

"Well, that wasn't very clever, was it? I suppose he signed the new one?"

"Yes, of course."

"And is it witnessed?"

"Yes, there are two witnesses."

"Who?"

"I'm afraid I am not at liberty to reveal..."

"Wait," Mother said, holding her palm towards him and looking up at the ceiling.

I leant in to take a closer look, "Someone called Stephen and... Good Lord... *Carl*. That must be Slim and Carl."

Mother lowered her hand and her eyes focused back on Simon, "Thank you, Simon. That wasn't so hard, was it?"

"What? But I didn't... Mrs Henderson, I must ask you to keep this information confidential for now," he said, dabbing at the moisture around his face with his shirt cuff.

"Oh, must you?" Mother said, rising from her seat and turning her back on him, before sailing from the room like the Empress I now saw her as.

# CHAPTER 21

When I got outside, Mother was sitting on a garden wall further down the street.

"Mother?"

"You were right," she said. "She killed you for your money."

I sat beside her, "I really can't believe it."

She turned towards my voice, "I can. Do you remember when I first met Becky and I told you that your auras were all to pot?"

"Yes."

"Becky's was brown, just plain brown."

"Which means what?"

"Greed and self-involvement."

I didn't know how to respond. I usually dismissed her talk of auras as ridiculous, but in my current state I was finding myself less swift to judge such matters.

"I'm hungry," Mother said and set off up the road.

I hurried to catch up with her, "Where are we going?"

"I thought that Café Amato was nice. What happened with Simon's phone, by the way? Nearly frightened me to death."

"You and me both. I don't know how it happened; I felt furious, lashed out and something let me connect with it."

She stopped suddenly, causing an elderly couple to bump into the back of her, "Oh, sorry, just had a thought. Do go by. Howard, maybe you can cross the divide when you're angry or feel really strong emotion? Do you think?"

The elderly couple moved on, seemingly unperturbed by a brightly coloured lady talking to herself in the street. It can't be uncommon in Bexhill, I suppose.

"It's possible, I'm still learning. I'm not sure I can do it again on demand, but it's worth monitoring."

I heard a cry from above like course laughter, and looked up to see my friendly seagull circling above us. I waved, instantly feeling foolish, but it circled once more and took off towards the sea. I wondered if its presence was a sign that I was still destined to be pulled back towards the stars at some point. I doubled my steps and caught up with Mother, "We need a plan. We have to stop her as soon as possible."

"Oh, I know that," she said. "Are you hungry? How do you eat, where you are?"

"I'm not sure I do. I haven't been hungry since it happened."

"That's not like you."

"I know, but I have this pleasant feeling of fullness, like I've eaten something absolutely delicious and don't want anything else."

"How lovely, and you won't get fat," she said, stopping

to flick a stone out of one of her jelly sandals.

"Mother, I'm already fat. That hasn't changed, unfortunately."

She dismissed me with a wave, "Puppy fat, it'll drop off."

"You've been saying that since I was six."

"You're just big boned."

I smiled at her, "You were always very kind about my weight."

She pulled a tissue from her bulging bag, "Don't be nice to me, especially now. I'm not used to it," she said. "Come on, I need some lunch, even if you don't."

We walked towards the shops. The bright sun on our backs warmed me, but I didn't even break a sweat. It was a rather pleasant sensation.

"Alright, let's focus on what to do next," I said, feeling the need for a list. "Let's recap;

1. Carl & Slim removed my existing will from home.

2. Someone, probably Becky, replaced it with one in her favour, written on paper from my house for authenticity. All with the connivance of Simon Moon.

3. Then Becky pushed me off the cliff.

"Do you think it was all planned in advance?" Mother said, avoiding a dog on an overlong lead.

"It would seem so. But do we have any concrete evidence we can present to the police?"

"We have a witness to Carl and Slim going into your

house."

"Mr Crawford, yes, that's a start. What else?"

"She must have forged your signature on the will. The police have people who can look at all that, don't they?"

"Yes, it's possible. Also, Simon Moon looked pretty close to cracking. If the police interrogate him, he might spill the beans."

"Good, so we're nearly there."

"But we still don't know who is ultimately responsible. Who is Seven? If he put Becky under so much pressure that she resorted to doing... that..."

Mother stopped and stepped to the side of the pavement, "You're going to have to say it, you know," she said, putting her hand out in front of her. "Put your hand in mine."

"Mother..."

"Do it," there was a tone in her voice that made me obey. "Is it there?"

"Yes."

"Good. Howard, you haven't actually said that she killed you. She did it, Howard. Your daughter is a murderer."

A wave of emotion flooded through me and I have never felt the need to cry so much, but the tears wouldn't come. Suddenly, I felt the warmth of the hand that held mine and I squeezed it.

"I felt it," Mother cried. "Did you squeeze my hand?"

"Yes."

"Do it again," she said, her eyes bright with excitement.

I tried, but that one touch had allowed the pent-up pain and hurt to dissipate, "I can't."

"Never mind, love. It was smashing."

"There's still a big part of me that can't believe she did it for her own reasons. I think I need to hear her tell me why. I have to understand."

"Right, then, that's what we'll do, we'll get her to confess," Mother said, banging the rubbish bin next to her with her fist and setting off at speed to the café.

It was strange to be back in Café Amato and clearly Mrs A hadn't heard the news about my demise, "On your own today? No Henderson or the young lady?" she asked, while serving Mother her egg and cress sandwich,

"Not today, no. What's going on outside?" Mother pointed to red and white barriers being erected along the pavement.

"Oh, they're getting ready for the Night Carnival later. It's a bit of a nuisance, but quite fun. It's for the children really. Enjoy your lunch," and she went back to the kitchen.

Mother spent a few minutes picking most of the cress out of the sandwich and I watched with my usual frustration, "If you don't want the cress, why ask for egg and cress?"

"Egg should come with cress, it's traditional, but it depends on my mood," was her explanation, which made no sense but this was not the time to argue.

"So, we need a plan. What are we going to do to get Becky to confess?"

"Well, first off, we need to find her. Can you pop off and see if she's at home?"

"I don't actually know where she lives, but I could try the garage and the beach hut, I suppose."

"Good idea, make yourself useful while I have this."

I stood up, "Right, back in a minute." I closed my eyes and conjured up the inside of the Marina Garage as I'd seen it on Tuesday afternoon. I stepped forward and opened my eyes to the gloom of the closed-up workshop, "Bingo!". I wondered if I would ever get bored of being able to leap from place to place? I hoped not.

The garage was empty, except for the Fiat Panda that still stood silently in the middle of the room, the only witness to the first time I met Becky as she faced Carl and the gun. Was that all a performance too? The beginning of the charade to get me to part with my money to help my troubled, long-lost daughter? I smiled as I remembered the noise of the shot ringing around the garage – I bet they hadn't expected me to actually shoot at them.

I closed my eyes again and thought back to the interior of the Lazy Dayz Beach Hut. When I arrived it only took a second to know that it too was empty. Wherever Becky was lying low, it was somewhere I had never been.

I could only have been gone from Café Amato a few minutes, but by the time I returned Mother had finished her sandwich and was counting out change onto the table, "I'm back," I said. "Have you finished already?"

"I was hungrier than I thought. Come on we need to get going," she said, pulling her bag over her shoulder. "Thank you for the sandwich, very nice," she called to Mrs

A as she stepped out of the café.

"Where are we going?"

"We're off to get reinforcements," she said, as she marched towards the seafront. "Any luck finding Becky?"

"No, she wasn't at either place. What reinforcements?"

Mother waved her hand in the air, in which she held the pink kitty phone, "Destiny awaits."

Ten minutes later she was sitting on a wooden crate in an empty flat, while Destiny stared at her clutching her own kitty phone to her chest, "I can't believe it. I can't believe they would actually kill him. This is just... awful. Mrs Henderson, I am so sorry."

"Thank you, dear, call me Sue. You have nothing to be sorry for, it's not your fault."

Destiny pulled another packing box alongside Mother's and sat down, "But he was trying to help me, may he rest in peace. How do you know that it was Becky who pushed him, if you weren't actually there?"

That was a good point, but the last thing we needed was for Mother to tell her the truth, "Don't tell her, Mother. She'll think you're potty."

Mother looked towards my voice, "But..."

"No, she will think you're crazy," I glanced at Destiny who was already looking at Mother with concern. "Just tell her I'm a witness who can't testify."

She frowned, then turned back to Destiny, "There was a witness, but they can't go to the police. It's a bit hard to explain, but they know for a fact that Becky pushed Howard to his death – they were there. We also have evidence that she has created a fake will, so that she inherits everything. That's why she did it."

"I see," Destiny said. "But I don't know what help I can be."

"If I can get Becky to talk to me and confess, I'm going to need a proper witness to what she says."

"Oh, Sue, I don't know. If she's killed once, won't you be in danger? Won't we both be?"

"We can't put her at risk, Mother, not with the baby," I said, now pacing the room trying to come up with a plan. "If you hadn't been in such a rush, we could have made a list of ideas in the café and sorted it out."

"I'm not rushing, we have to move fast before the police call it suicide and she scarpers with the money," she said, looking at Destiny instead of me.

"I understand that," Destiny said. "It's all such a shock. Your phone call, then your son's death..."

"That's it" I said. "The phone, you could record the conversation with Becky on the phone. Switch it on and put it in your bag."

"Yes, I've seen it done on the telly."

"Pardon, Sue?"

Mother shook her head, "Sorry, love, just thinking out loud. I do that a lot; you'll get used to it. I was just thinking, instead of you being there I could record Becky's confession with my phone... but you might have to show me how to do it."

"Oh, I see, yes, I could do that. But you'd still be putting yourself in danger."

"Don't you worry about me - you'll understand, the moment you see your little one. You'll become a lioness and fear no one where your children are concerned. Destiny, I know you think you could lose your husband if everything comes out..." She looked at her intently, "But whatever happens you will survive and you will still have your child, but my son is dead because of these people. I will not let them get away with it and I certainly don't want anyone else to die. We have to put a stop to this."

Destiny stared at her and looked down at her baby bump, "You're right. I can't let anyone else suffer, that is not what I believe in. What's your plan?"

Mother sat back, "My plan? Good point. What's the plan?"

I stepped up beside them, "We need to smoke Becky and Seven out from wherever they're hiding."

"Yes, that's it," Mother said, then smiled at Destiny. "We need to smoke and get them out in the open."

"By smoking?" Destiny said.

"By bluffing them," I said quickly in Mother's ear.

"By bluffing them."

"I think Destiny needs to text Seven..."

Mother nodded, as if thinking the plan through in her head, "I think you need to text Seven..."

"Okay," Destiny said, pulling her kitty phone from her handbag. "What should I say?"

"I'm getting to that bit, just give me a moment," Mother said, rising from her box and stretching her legs. "You've got his number, haven't you?"

"Yes, he sends me messages when he wants something."

I then relayed the plan to Mother that had started to form in my head, and she repeated it to Destiny, "You need to tell him that you have evidence to prove that a man was murdered last night on Galley Hill by someone from The Seven. You have to insist on meeting tonight... at the...erm, where?... oh yes, the De La Warr Pavilion."

"But how do we know he'll come?" Destiny asked. "He might just send those two men. Carl, is it? And the big one."

"He might, but then we use plan B, which is..?"

I prompted her again, "If Carl and Slim come, we'll leave them at the meeting point. When they get fed-up, we follow them and hope they lead us to either Seven or Becky. Plan A is that Seven turns up himself. Plan C is that Becky is the one who comes. If so, we know that she and Seven are actually in cahoots or how else would she know about the meet?"

"You'll have to go more slowly than that," she said.

Eventually, having fed the information to Mother in bite sized pieces we got the plan across to Destiny.

"It actually feels good to be taking back control," she said. "What do we do when we finally find Seven or Becky?"

"Leave that to me," Mother said. "Your job is to send the messages and get them to come to the meeting. Tell him nine o'clock tonight. Can you be there to watch out for who's coming? The De La Warr Pavilion is on a corner, so we need to watch for them from different directions."

"Yes, Mark, my husband, has a church meeting tonight, so I can slip away."

"Excellent," she pulled the crumpled newspaper pages from her bag. "Here's a photo of Inspector Ellis, who we think might be Seven, so you can spot him. You can't miss Becky, she's tall, thin with silver hair, and lots of earrings. Oh, and she wears a leather jacket and rides an old motorbike."

"Right, I'll send the message now, then I'd better get back to the office. They'll be wondering where I am."

"Of course," Mother said, holding her arms out as Destiny stood. "You are being very brave."

Destiny fought back tears, "Not as brave as you," and they hugged.

I watched with pride as these two, very different women prepared to risk their own futures to avenge my death.

# CHAPTER 22

I watched the half-light of evening throw strange shadows across the bold curves of the De La Warr Pavilion's façade, as the Night Carnival passed in front of it. People paraded in bright costumes with lit torches, children screamed with excitement, and lengths of coloured bulbs swung between lampposts in the evening breeze, as marshals scurried about like dayglow beetles in their high visibility vests.

It was strange to be in the midst of it all, yet apart from it. I could simply stand back and watch from afar, something I'd been trying to do all my life, perhaps.

However, contemplation of my new invisibility didn't last long, as the matter in hand was more pressing. We had no idea who was coming, as Destiny hadn't had a reply after texting Seven, but her phone showed that the message had been received and read. She was outside Café Amato, keeping an eye to the west along the promenade. Mother was on the eastern end of the Pavilion's car park, looking down the parade route. As it neared the time of the rendezvous, we just had to wait and see who, if anyone, would show up.

Despite the sense of calm that surrounded me in my new state, I was nervous. No further harm could be done to me, of that I was sure, but we had no idea how this would go. Mother was insistent that she had no interest in treading carefully, she wanted Becky and Seven to face the full consequences of their actions, regardless of the risk to her. Destiny had also embraced the warrior spirit and was ready to fight her way to freedom from The Seven. She had even taken it upon herself to ask her husband, who happened to be the police chaplain, to try and get information on the background to the Inspector Ellis corruption story. She hadn't told him the real reason why, of course.

I was beside Destiny when she received a text from Mother. I read it over her shoulder;

Any word from your husband, about policeman or his dead friend?

Destiny replied; Not yet. Will let you know. Xx

I'd mastered the art of moving between the lookouts, by pulling up images of each location in my mind and taking a step in their direction. In an instant I could pop up beside them. It was not entirely necessary, to go back and forth so frequently, but it was peculiarly exciting. This whole afterlife business I had poo-pood for so long, certainly had elements that were appealing. In many ways it seemed preferable to the slow decline I had been facing.

I returned to Mother. She was stalking impatiently up and down behind the crowd that was now several people deep at the barrier. They had begun to cheer the Salvation Army Band and I paused for a moment to watch them; I never could resist the sound of a good brass band. When they had passed, I looked around for Mother and caught a flash of her pink pinafore and bright white hair far up the road. I headed after her, "Where are you off to?" I said into her ear, making her stagger into a man with a child dressed as a ghost on his shoulders.

"You'll be the death of me," she said, pushing herself back into the throng. "I'm going to have to hang a bell round your neck, so I get some warning."

"Why are you all the way up here?"

"I can't just stand around; I need to keep on the move. If she's coming this way, I'll spot her early and be ready."

"Becky might not come," I said. "It's a risk for her."

"She'll come, I know it. She'll want to clear up the mess she's made. Women are like that... even the evil ones."

"If you say so."

The local animal rescue centre float was passing by, with gyrating people dressed as dogs, cats and a giant turkey, for some reason.

"There," I shouted.

"Where?" Mother said, jumping up to try and see over the crowd.

"Walking with the parade, on the far side. I'm sure that was Becky, she's trying to hide among the group of dogs, next to the lorry."

"I can't see," Mother said and started to wade through the packed bodies, pushing people aside. "Old woman coming through," she yelled, as she forced her way closer. When she got to the barrier the float had passed by on its slow journey, so she forced the barriers apart and started to squeeze through.

A marshal in his dayglow vest stepped in front of her, "No, no. Performers and paraders only."

"You're here," Mother shouted.

The marshal scratched his beard, "Erm, performers and paraders and official marshals only," he said.

"But..."

"No buts, madam. We have rules, please return behind the erected safety barrier."

Fortunately, the cheers of the crowd drowned out Mother's reply, but she was duly returned to behind the barrier by the officious marshal. She tried to move down the parade route but there were too many people, so she retreated back to the pavement behind them and started to canter towards the pavilion.

"Can you see her?" she shouted.

"Yes, she's still with the animals, but they've stopped. There's a bit of a logjam up ahead."

Her own path was impeded by the man carrying his child wearing a sheet over him like Caspar, the ghost. She looked up at the little ghost, then dived into her tote bag and drew out her purse.

"How much for the costume?" she said to the man.

"Pardon?"

"The ghost costume. I want to buy it."

He lifted the child off his shoulders and stood him on the ground, "Why?"

Mother gave one of her best impish smiles, "It's a surprise for a friend. She scares easily."

The man laughed, "I'm not sure. Robin enjoys being a ghost."

"One hundred pounds," she said, drawing out the notes.

"How much?"

She counted out her remaining cash, "One hundred and seventy-five, final offer."

The man snatched the sheet, with black netting eyes, off young Robin and gave it to Mother, "Deal," he said.

She handed over the money as Robin began to bawl, "I'll get you a hot dog," the father said, pocketing the cash and moving away quickly, in case the mad old woman changed her mind.

Mother threw the sheet over her head and ploughed back to the barrier, eased her way through and faced the marshal again, "Performer coming through," she said.

"Who are you with?" he said.

"Ghostbusters," she said without hesitation, and headed off down the road, waving at the cheering crowd.

I looked around for Becky, but couldn't see her. I tried to pass through the crowd, but, as with attempting to get through the door, I was constantly blocked. I stood still and to my surprise the sea of people seemed to be able to move effortlessly around me, never once touching me or walking through the space I occupied. Why then did it not work the other way? I tried again to walk forwards, but every time a living body blocked my path I could go no further.

Instead, I conjured up an image of the animal rescue float – and in a moment I was there, right beside it. A giant dog danced alongside me, his huge ears bouncing. On the other side of him was Becky.

She was almost within touching distance. She couldn't see me, but I wondered if she could sense my presence as she turned a full circle, her eyes darting left and right. She didn't look like the confident woman I had known; her face was tense and pale under her steely hair – she looked like a haunted woman. Which, of course, she now was.

The parade started to move off and I stepped close to her and she shivered, glancing over her shoulder. As she did so, she and I both heard a single word cutting through the music and cheers, "Killer."

She stopped and spun around, her eyes wildly searching the crowd and the dancers. There it was again, "Killer.". She couldn't identify the source of the cry, but I could. A small, child-sized ghost, white sheet flapping above a pair of purple glitter jelly sandals, was about ten paces behind us and closing.

"Mother," I shouted. "Tell her 'Daddy-Dearest says, hello'."

"What?" I heard her shout, as she was grabbed by a large ginger kitten and waltzed into the middle of the road.

I kept my eye on Becky, who was still staying close to the lorry, which blocked her from the Pavilion side of the street.

I heard a muffled "Oof," and turned to see the ginger kitten lying in the road, holding its groin and rolling about.

The little ghost raced past me and dodged the giant

gyrating turkey.

"Mother," I shouted again, as I came up behind her. "Mother, tell her, 'Daddy-Dearest says hello'."

The ghost turned slightly then slowed, a few paces behind Becky, "Becky, Becky...".

As Becky turned to see the source of the voice, the ghost began to dance with the turkey. As Becky faced front again, Mother called, "Daddy-dearest says, hello."

Bingo! Becky stumbled as she frantically looked about for the source of the voice.

"Tell her, 'the job is not quite done', call her 'Daughter-Dearest'."

Mother had moved amongst the human-sized cats by now, "Becky, the job isn't done yet... daughter-dearest."

"What?" Becky yelled. "Who said that?" She started to run, nearly fell, corrected herself and took off down the parade, the little ghost hot on her heels. It must have been quite a sight - a young woman in leather jacket and jeans, being chased by a tiny ghost in plastic sandals – and the crowd went wild, cheering and applauding the pantomime.

Becky raced towards the De La Warr Pavilion, dodged through a barrier, barged onlookers out of the way and then shouldered through the door of the foyer. Being smaller, Mother had less success getting through the crowd, but finally she made it, puffing up the steps. The large glass and metal doors were heavy and she struggled to open them.

"I can't, Howard," she said, in defeat. "I can't do it."

"Take a moment," I said. "I'll find her." I peered through

the glass windows into the foyer, then closed my eyes, conjured up the image again in my mind and stepped forward. I was quickly transported to a display stand in the foyer, behind which Becky was crouching, still panting from her run. I could see Mother through the glass door, leaning on it to catch her breath. Then Destiny appeared beside her and I hurried across the foyer.

"Are you alright, Sue?" I heard Destiny say through the door.

The ghost nodded, "Yes, ta. How did you know it was me?"

"I saw a woman with silver hair running, then I saw the pink of your dress under the sheet and your sandals."

"She's behind the display of leaflets on the right," I called to Mother. "Take care."

"Stay here," Mother ordered and, with Destiny's help, she pushed open the door. She set off into the foyer, stopping in the middle. "Killer!" she called.

Nothing happened.

"Show yourself, Becky."

There was a moment's silence, then Becky took off across the polished floor and up the twisting staircase at the end of the foyer.

"Not more running," Mother sighed and started after her.

I was quicker than her in my new state, so stayed close on Becky's heels, as she took the stairs two at a time. She pounded her way up to the second floor, and there she continued across the landing to another flight of service stairs next to the lift. I thought for a moment that she was going to head back down, but instead she swerved and headed upwards. I shouted behind me to Mother, who was just cresting the steel and stone spiral stairs, "This way, up the stairs by the lift."

"More flipping stairs," she huffed, giving a couple leaving the toilets a shock as the small ghost charged across the floor.

I followed Becky up two more flights of stairs, Mother doing well to keep going behind us, all be it more slowly. At the top were three white doors, all shut. Becky immediately went to the one on the left, pushed the emergency bar and disappeared, the door slamming behind her.

A few moments later, Mother came up beside me, "Howard?" she said, breathing heavily.

"Are you okay?" I asked. "Do you need to rest?"

"Of course I need a rest. I'm over seventy and have just climbed Mount Kilimanjaro. But I'm not stopping now, where is she?"

"Through the door on the left," I said. "But..."

Before I could go on, Mother had yanked open the door and was through it.

"Wait!" I called, as the door swung too in front of me. "Damn it!".

It hadn't quite closed, but the gap was so tiny a mouse couldn't get through, let alone me. I stepped back, but I couldn't pull up an image of what was through the door - I'd never been here before. Mother was on her own.

Behind me I could sense someone approaching and turned to see Destiny creeping slowly up the stairs. Her tread was tentative and her hand held protectively over her tummy.

"Come on, Destiny, come on," I said, under my breath, as she crept towards me. She hesitated at the top of the stairs and looked at the three doors.

"This one, this one," I hissed, moving to stand against the door I needed her to open, but she turned to the one on the right. "No, no," I quickly moved to her side and she shivered, twisting left to where I stood. She hesitated, frowned and then approached the door to the left, noticing that it was slightly ajar.

She reached out to the push bar and gave it a gentle shove, just as the sound of a gunshot flew through the air.

# CHAPTER 23

With the sound of the shot ringing in my ears, Destiny screamed and I burst through the gap in the door she held open, just before she let it slam behind her. To my relief Mother stood in front of me on the roof of the building, still dressed as the little ghost, "Are you alright?".

She took hold of the sheet and pulled it slowly from her head, letting it fall to the ground, "Possibly not," she said, looking past me.

I turned. The first thing I saw was the gun – the same one I had used to shoot Carl, but this time the hand holding it was Becky's.

Becky stepped forward, her feet crunching on the gravel that was spread across the open expanse of roof. On one side of us we could hear the joyful sounds of carnival continuing far below, and the other side was the dark expanse of the English Channel stretching towards France, looking cold and dangerous.

Becky reached behind her to feel for the wall. She'd moved out of reach, so stepped back slightly until she could touch it, "Sorry I can't come over for a chat, but I have a small issue with heights," she said. "I'll let the bullet do the travelling if it has to." She stretched her arm out straight, taking aim, "You, Destiny, move over with the old woman."

"How did you know my name?" Destiny said, moving slowly to Mother.

"I've seen you plenty of times, when I was selling the drugs at your houses."

"You *sell* them?" I said.

"I thought you only did the deliveries, not actually sold them?" Mother said. "You can go to prison for a long time for that, Becky... not as long as for murder, but..."

"Shut up," Becky snapped.

I tensed, but Mother seemed untroubled as she continued softly, "Rebecca, what on earth have you got yourself into?"

"It's Becky, and it's nothing I can't handle."

"But more murders? That's going to be ever so hard to cover up. Your own father and then your grandmother? And a pregnant vicar's wife too?"

Becky's laugh was hard and tight, "Ha! An ex-con who's lied all her life? As for him, he wasn't my real father, like you're not my real granny."

"What?" I said, shock hitting me like a bullet. I stepped back sharply, the gravel shifting beneath my feet. I looked down at it and with vicious anger I kicked out, sending a spray of tiny pebbles towards Becky. She gasped, falling back against the wall.

Mother looked around her, "Was that you, Howard?" she whispered. "Howard?"

"Yes," I said. "It's just... I mean, I really thought she was..."

"I know, love, I know," she said, before turning sharply to Becky. "How could you be so cruel? You took advantage of him when he was at his lowest. He'd lost his wife, he knew he was going to die. He was alone and scared and you thought that made him an easy target, is that it? You don't have a decent bone in your body. You haven't just *killed* Howard, you've hurt him deeply."

Becky shrugged, pointing the gun back at Mother, "Nah, he never knew I wasn't his daughter. He died happy, well happier than you'd ever made him."

"Don't you dare," Mother yelled. "Don't you dare say that. He may be dead, but of course he's hurt. He loved you, you stupid girl. Why him? Why did you have to pick on my Howard? He never did anyone any harm."

"He had money, pots of it. He was on his way out. So, I just brought things forward a bit."

"How did you know?" I asked, and Mother repeated my question.

"We have our sources."

"Of course, Simon Moon. He was the only one who knew about my diagnosis and the size of my estate," again Mother repeated my words.

"Clever," Becky said to Mother. "That's pretty much it. The letter and poor long lost daughter act got Henderson here easily. He fell for it; poor little me caught in this awful situation, up to my ears in pretend debt. Pile on the pressure, get him chased all over town until he didn't know what to do with himself. He was supposed to cough up some cash to help me – well, he was too tight fisted for that, wasn't he? Eventually he offered me a stupid loan, never even thought of putting me in his will, did he?"

Mother's voice was tight and angry, "So, you killed him and switched the wills."

"Ooh, you do know a lot, don't you? Yep, the original plan was to get a chunk of cash up front and if it was big enough, leave it at that. Getting some more from the will when he croaked would have been a bonus. We were prepared to wait a bit while the cancer did its thing, as long as he didn't take too long to die. But then he announced that he was going to give the treatment a go, and try and live as long as he could – maybe I was too good at being the loving daughter? Anyway, I had no choice then. He pretty much signed his own death warrant."

"So, none of it was real? Not even The Seven?" I asked, through Mother.

"That's real enough. We've been running those scams for a while, but they weren't bringing in enough. We've been waiting for something bigger. Once his money comes through, we're off. Canada, maybe. That always looks nice."

"We?" Mother said. "Who's we? Who is Seven?"

Becky pushed away from the wall, "You and your obsession with Seven..."

Before she could say anymore the door beside her burst open and the enormous bulk of Slim followed by Carl charged towards us. The door swung back with such force that it knocked the gun out of Becky's hand. She staggered sideways and with a terrifying scream disappeared over the edge of the roof.

Carl and Slim heard her go and ran to where she had stood. I did the same, peering down into the darkness at the back of the building. Becky hadn't fallen all the way to the ground, but her body was spread-eagled on the roof of the café two floors below us, a drop of at least thirty feet. We were all startled by the cry of a seagull as it swooped past us and down towards the body, landing at its side.

"Shoo, shoo," Slim called, waving his hands.

"Leave it," Carl said. "She's gone, she won't be bothered."

I slowly walked away from the edge of the roof. I was numb. Mother had lost her son at the hands of Becky, and now I had lost my daughter because of her too. The fact that she hadn't existed in the first place didn't make it any easier. I had loved her and had loved the purpose that being a father gave me.

"So, is she dead?" Mother's voice woke us all from our shock.

"Yeah," Carl said, turning.

"Good."

"Mother!"

While we had been focusing on Becky, Mother had retrieved the fallen gun and was standing with feet apart pointing it firmly with both hands.

"Now then, gentlemen, I think you have some explaining to do," she said. "Destiny, please go back downstairs and wait for us in the foyer. Have a rest. We'll be down in a minute."

Destiny didn't move, "But..."

"No buts, young lady, off you go."

This time Destiny did as she was asked, closing the door to the roof gently but not completely behind her.

"Right, time to talk, boys, or you are going the same way as her," Mother said, her voice taking on a slight hint of an American drawl.

Carl sneered at her, "I don't think so, old lady. There are no bullets in that gun."

We all ducked as she fired into the air and the noise ricocheted off the walls and buildings around us. There was a scream then a big cheer and laughter from the carnival below.

"Doesn't sound like it's empty to me," Mother said, looking proud of herself.

"I didn't say it was empty," Carl said, having moved in front of Slim. "I said there were no *bullets*... no real bullets. They're blanks; we've never had any live ammo."

"So, Howard didn't really shoot you in the garage?"

Slim giggled behind Carl, "Nah, that was all an act. Part of the hustle to get his money."

"Fire at them," I yelled to Mother, furious with my own stupidity and their glee at the deception.

"What?" she said.

"Fire at the ground in front of them on three. One, two, three..."

On cue, Mother fired at their feet and I took an enormous swipe at the gravel beside them letting all my pent-up anger and frustration spray it into the air. They screamed and clung to each other.

Mother laughed, "Seems like someone found some real bullets."

"No, no," Carl said, looking horrified. "There were never supposed to be proper guns that could kill people. We wouldn't ever... she promised."

"Who? Who promised?" Mother snapped.

"The boss. Our job was to frighten people, we never actually did anything, just pretended."

"Yeah, pretended," Slim said, his voice shaking.

"But Becky killed my son!"

Carl put his hands up in the air, "That wasn't supposed to happen. We didn't know she was going to do that."

Slim also held his shivering hands aloft, "Yeah, we couldn't believe it, could we, babe?"

"Wait, wait," I said, everything becoming clearer and yet more convoluted. "Are you saying you were all carrying out Seven's plan, but Becky went rogue?"

Mother relayed my question.

"She didn't follow the plan," Carl said. "She was bonkers, always going off and doing her own thing."

"Who's the boss, then? We know he's called Ellis," Mother said, flicking the barrel of the gun at them.

Slim giggled, "How does she know that?"

Carl shrugged, "Dunno."

Mother was losing patience, "Howard told me that when he thought he'd shot you in the garage, you shouted to call Ellis. We've tracked down Dave Ellis, is it him?"

"No, no – I see what you've done there, but it's not *Ellis*,"

Carl said. "It's LS, the letters L and S."

"Fine, so they're initials, but who for," Mother said, waving the gun at them to speed things up, and their flailing hands rose high in the air again.

"Alright, alright. LS is what we call his mother," Carl said, gesturing to Slim. "Laughing Skirt. Every time she laughs her fat stomach makes her skirt bounce up and down, so we call her Laughing Skirt. LS for short."

Slim sniggered again, "Stupid fat cow."

Mother turned the focus of the gun on Slim alone, "That's no way to talk about your mother," she told him.

"She ain't my real mother, she's my step-mother. She's the one got us into all this. Can I put my hands down, my arms are aching?"

"Yes, fine, but only if you tell us the whole story."

Slim looked at Carl, who shrugged and lowered his arms.

"I was born on August the twelfth..." Slim began.

"Not that much of the story," Mother said. "More recent."

"Oh, right, well, my real mum died when I was a kid. Dad went off the rails a bit, so I did too, getting into trouble at school, all that lot. Then, he got remarried - to Laughing Skirt. At first, it was fine, Dad seemed happier."

"He was always into dodgy stuff, though," Carl added.

"Oh, yeah, kickbacks here, pulling in favours there, all that lot. They started to get me involved when I was older, just frightening people really, cos of my size. Then I met Carl," Slim gave him a crooked smile and blushed a deep red across his large, round cheeks.

Carl straightened his usually stooped posture, "You might as well know, we're together," he said, looking at Mother defiantly and deliberately taking Slim's great big hand in his small one.

Mother shrugged, "So? You're looking in the wrong place for sympathy here. I was devastated when Howard came out as straight. I was convinced he was gay; I had all sorts of plans for us."

Well, that was news to me, but a discussion for other times.

Carl looked surprised, "Well, his step-mum didn't think like that. She caught us together, swore blind that if his dad found out he'd kill Slim. She threatened to tell him. That's why we do all this bad stuff, to keep her quiet. But we've never really hurt anyone."

"We wouldn't," Slim said, with a sniff. "We've got a cat."

"I'm really sorry about your son," Carl said, looking genuinely upset.

Slim shook his head slowly, "Yeah, that wasn't right,"

They looked pathetic standing side by side, holding hands, both staring at the ground like schoolboys who had been up to no good.

"So, they were being blackmailed too, like Destiny and Adam," I said.

Mother's phone pinged, "Do you think I should check that?"

Carl and Slim both shrugged as I answered her, "Yes, it might be Seven."

"Fine, sit on the ground, you two. I'll have this gun back on you by the time you've stood up again, understand?"

They both nodded and flopped onto the gravel, while Mother retrieved her pink kitty phone, "Oh, it's a text from Destiny, hang on. She says, Mark - that's her husband, I think, the vicar – Mark says, the dead policeman was called Tony Amato, he was Dave Ellis' partner for a while."

"Tony Amato?" Slim said. "What's that about my dad?"

"Was he a policeman who died in a car accident?" Mother asked.

Slim nodded, "Yeah, a couple of years ago. But Laughing Skirt said she knows too much about all the bad things we've done. She told us we'd both go to prison if we ever squealed or left her."

"Cow," Carl added, looking miserable and clinging to Slim's hand for comfort.

I couldn't believe what I was hearing, "Mrs A?"

"So, your Step-Mother is Laughing Skirt, who is actually Mrs Amato, who is Mrs A, who runs the café over there?" Mother pointed from the roof down to the seafront parade of shops.

They both nodded.

Mother waved the gun in the air triumphantly, "I knew I wasn't wrong about her aura."

"Where does Becky come into it?" I asked.

"Oh, yes," Mother said. "What about Becky? Who does she belong to?"

Slim frowned, "She's Laughing Skirt's daughter, my

step-sister."

Things were moving so fast and everything seemed to be changing like tides washing around rock pools. At the top of this pyramid of chaos and human misery was the charming Mrs A. I found it hard to believe and yet here it was laid out before me.

"They have got to go to the police, tell them everything they've told us," I said.

"I know, but they've suffered too."

"They have to talk to the police, how else are we going to put a stop to Mrs A?" I said.

"Easy, now we've got this gun we go and get her and march her into the police station. We tell them all about it, they can interrogate her; they're already looking into her husband's crimes."

"She's gone," Slim said, suddenly. "Carl, Carl, she's gone."

We both turned to see him on all fours peering over the edge of the roof, then ran to see for ourselves. Where Becky's body had lain there was now just scuffed gravel and a small pool of dark blood.

# CHAPTER 24

"Come on, we have to find her," Mother shouted and ran towards the door to the stairs.

Carl and Slim started to scramble to their feet, "Not you two," I said, forgetting myself.

Mother skidded to a halt, "No, not you two. Right come here, the pair of you." She stood with her hands on her hips, a familiar pose from my childhood I had forgotten until now. Carl and Slim shuffled over to stand in front of her, both towering above her tiny frame, "I am going to give you the choice I used to give Howard. One, you can either do the right thing, tell the truth, take your punishment and move on. Or two, you can do the wrong thing and live with the consequences for the rest of your lives. In your case, that will be looking over your shoulder for the police and me. So, which is it to be? Actually, forget that, I don't have time for all this, sit back on the ground."

They did as they were told.

"Now, you can sit there and think about your behaviour. When you've decided what to do, you can go. So, we'll either see you at the police station or on a wanted poster. It's up to you. If you really want to be free to live your lives, I think you know what you have to do." With that she popped the gun in her patchwork tote, pulled open the door to the stairwell and marched off the roof, leaving Carl and Slim sitting stunned on the gravel.

I felt like applauding, she was magnificent. As I'd grown up, a sensitive boy with an overactive mother, we had grown further and further apart. I kept her at arm's length, mortified at being the centre of attention whenever she was around. In doing so, I had failed to notice how truly original my mother was, something I should have celebrated not been embarrassed by.

Carl looked at Slim, "You okay?"

Slim sniffed, "Yeah, you?"

"Not bad. Looks like Laughing Skirt's for it."

"I know... us too."

I left them to their deliberations and took the short cut by picturing the theatre foyer in my mind. As I arrived, Mother came panting down the stairs, "Have you seen Becky?" she asked Destiny, who was sitting on a bench by the front doors.

"No," Destiny said. "She was... I mean, she fell off the roof. Isn't she dead?"

"Hm, she wasn't as dead as we thought and now she's vanished."

"Oh, my goodness, this just gets worse and worse."

"I know it's all been a shock for you," Mother said, rubbing Destiny's arm soothingly. "But we need you to stay strong for a little bit longer. Can you keep watch on Café Amato, over the road? We need to know where the woman who runs it is."

"Mrs A? She's very nice, she does a cake stall for the church fair."

"Well, she won't be baking for much longer. It turns out that she is Seven."

Destiny gasped, "No!"

"Trust me, Mrs A's responsible for everything, especially Becky – she's her daughter."

"That's incredible," Destiny said, rubbing her tummy.

"I know, but she was married to the crooked policeman that died, he set all this up. Carl and Slim just told us everything."

"It's all so incredible, in quiet Bexhill of all places. Well, at least you have their confessions now and Becky's..."

"Oh, for f..."

"Mother!" I said, intercepting the language.

"I completely forgot. When she trapped me on the roof, I wasn't ready. Then she fell off and those two boys arrived... it put it all out of my mind. I didn't record any of it."

"But you have Carl and Slim. Do you think they'll turn against her?"

"I'm pretty sure they will, they're good boys really. But we can't take that chance, we have to find Becky. I need you to keep an eye on Mrs A, and if she moves let me know where she goes. Don't put yourself in danger though, call the police if you have to."

"Yes, that's fine," Destiny said. "So, where's Becky gone?"

Mother stamped her foot, "Oh, poop, hang on," she

swung round and headed for the stairs again.

I called after her, "Take the lift, Mother. I don't want you keeling over."

"That's your best idea yet," she said and swerved towards it. "Apart from the gravel and the blank bullet, that was pretty good too."

Destiny stared at her, "Are you alright, Sue?"

"Hm, oh yes, just... well, I'm talking to Howard, but don't worry. Off you go and keep an eye on the café."

Destiny watched Mother get in the lift, and shook her head sadly as she made her way outside to start her surveillance duties.

As we rode up to the top floor, Mother's small eyes, magnified by her huge glasses, were alive with passion and righteous indignation. I had never felt so proud of her, "I'm sorry, Mum."

"Mum? You never call me Mum. What are you sorry for?"

"Not trusting you or trying to understand you. Not getting to know you properly, I suppose. I actually think you are amazing and I wish I'd been more like you. I think my life would have been quite different if I had. It's funny how similar Maggie was to you, in a way. I hadn't seen it before, but you both have this strength to be yourselves that I never had. It drove me mad in you when I was young, but in her it was, well, I thought it was magnificent. You're magnificent too. So, I'm sorry."

She didn't move as the lift chugged its way upward, but stared at the floor in silence. After a moment we shuddered to a halt and with a ping the doors opened. I stepped out and turned, but Mother remained where she was.

"Are you coming?" I asked.

She nodded and came onto the landing, "Howard, that is the nicest thing that anyone has ever said to me. I don't know what to say."

"Would you like a hug?"

She gasped, "Really? Oh, Howard..." and she began to cry.

Seeing this tiny woman, standing alone, weeping at the simple idea of a hug I should have given her years ago when I was able to, nearly broke my heart. I felt a warm tear roll down my cheek and I knew that I could do it. I moved to her and wrapped my arms around her. The sensation was extraordinary. I could feel her tiny frame within my arms, but I could also feel the warmth and softness of her.

"Howard, I can feel you," she whispered.

"I know, Mum. I know."

We stood together for what seemed like ages, but could only have been a minute, before I felt her slipping away and I could no longer feel her properly. Then I heard a distant sound, like a single note from a flute, and a gentle breeze started to lap around me. Is this what I'd been brought back for? To hug my mother? Was this the unfinished business that had given me a brief reprieve from wherever I was going next?

I began to sense my connection to the ground loosening, "No, no. She still needs me." I couldn't speak the words out loud, but my head resounded with them,

"Please, a little longer. Let me finish this."

Gradually, the flute faded away, the breeze subsided and I felt the floor beneath my feet again, "Thank you," I whispered.

"You're welcome," Mother said, wiping her eyes. "My boy, I do love you."

"And I you, Mum."

"Right, Howard, shall we finish this?"

I held my breath, knowing that once this business with The Seven was finished I would almost certainly have to leave.

"Howard?"

"I'm here. Yes, let's do this."

❊ ❊ ❊

Out on the now dark roof, Carl and Slim were still sitting quietly together on the ground.

"One more thing," Mother said, as we barged through the door from the stairwell. "Where would Becky go if she was on the run? Where will I find her?"

Slim scrunched up his face and chewed his cheek, Carl scratched his elbow.

"Well?"

"I'm pretty sure she stashed stuff at her beach hut," Slim said, slowly. "Her Emergency Parachute she called it. She might go there."

"Excellent," Mother said. "You see, you can do the right thing."

"We've decided," Carl said. "We're going to the police station."

Mother beamed at them, "Good boys, I knew you weren't really bad kids."

We left them there, like two puppies who had learnt to sit when asked and had received their first treat. I couldn't help but feel for them.

Back on the street, as the last floats of the carnival were slowly passing by, Destiny was on guard opposite Café Amato.

"We'll be back as soon as we can," Mother said to her.

Destiny looked back into the foyer, "We? Who's going with you?"

"Howard, of course, he's always with me."

She smiled, "Of course, he is. He'll always be with you, Sue, in your heart."

"The town's packed," I said. "We'll never get a taxi."

"We'll have to steal a car then," Mother said.

"Sorry, what was that?" Destiny asked.

"We've got to get out to Becky's beach hut, we need a car."

"Take mine," she said, pulling her keys from her handbag.

"That's very kind... Adam!"

Destiny blinked, trying to follow her train of thought, but already Mother was off down the steps waving wildly, "Adam, over here."

A familiar dark hooded figure, in skinny jeans was

sloping along the pavement, he either couldn't hear Mother's cries or chose to ignore them. She was not to be put off though and when she thumped him on the back he nearly tipped into the gutter, ripping the headphones from his ears, "Friggin' hell woman, what you doing?"

"I've been shouting at you, Adam. Don't you remember me? I'm Howard's mother."

"Howard?"

"Well, he prefers Henderson."

He nodded warily, "Yes, I remember."

"Adam, it's a very long story, which we don't have time for, but we know who Seven is and, don't be shocked, but Becky is not who she says she is. She's one of them. She killed Henderson, she pushed him off a cliff. We didn't know how to get hold of you, but Destiny, the estate agent, has been helping," she waved vaguely behind her.

"It's complicated, but we have to stop Becky. I can't do it alone... well, I'm not alone, but that's even more complicated. We think she's at the beach hut, will you come with me?"

"Frigg me," he said, looking paler than usual.

"Will you come with me, Adam?"

"Yeah, okay. Don't know what you want me to do though?"

"Just provide back up, that's all."

"K, whatever," he said.

Mother patted him on the arm and he flinched, "Good for you, Adam. We need to get going." She turned round and shouted back, "Where's the car, Destiny?"

"Only round the corner by the park. White VW Golf, just click the key thing and the lights will flash," she called. "Good luck. I'll let you know if anything happens here."

"I'm going to hop straight to where Becky is," I said.

Mother shifted her tote bag to the other shoulder, "Hang on, hang on, Howard. You could have found out where she was just now!"

"Are you alright?" Adam said, his eyes wide.

"Just a minute, Adam, please" Mother said. "Howard, I went all the way back up to those boys and you could have just popped off and found her."

"Technically, yes," I said. "But only if I'd been there before."

"You've been to the beach hut, though."

"I know... I forgot."

"You are supposed to be the sensible one in our family, Howard."

"What are you doing?" Adam said, backing slowly away.

"I'm talking to Howard," Mother said. "He may be dead, but he can still be really annoying." She tucked her arm into Adam's and started to lead him away, "Come on, you know where the beach hut is, don't you?"

"Yeah," he said, trying to remove himself from Mother's vice-like grip with little success.

I closed my eyes, blotting out the noise and lights of the parade and focused on the Lazy Dayz Beach Hut. Before I knew it, I was back on the beach with little yellow hut in front of me. The sudden darkness was disorientating for a moment, but I quickly recovered and found myself able to see quite clearly through the gloom. A slim line of dull light shone around the wooden doors, to show someone was inside.

There was a flutter of wings as my familiar seagull landed heavily on the roof, it gave me a swift nod and settled down for what looked like a nap. The noise of its arrival sent up a muffled cry from inside and Becky's bruised face popped out of the half-open doorway. The moonlight was enough to see that the right side of her face was swollen and her once silver hair was matted with dried blood.

"Anyone there?" she croaked, flinching as the words opened a cut on her lip. She waited for a reply, but when none came, she retreated back inside.

I moved easily across the pebbles, which was a pleasant change, and onto the terrace. In a peculiar repetition of our first meeting, I slipped through the open door and stood in the shadows created by the low powered battery lamp, and looked at this person as if for the first time.

She had moved all the furniture to one side and lifted several of the planks from the floor. Kneeling beside the hole, she was reaching around with one hand and pulling out clear-plastic wrapped bundles of cash. Her movements were jerky and impeded by her right arm, which she kept tucked close to her body. It looked broken from the way she was holding herself.

As she struggled, I knew that I felt nothing for her now. She wasn't the daughter I had grown to love over the few days we had shared together. This woman was a stranger and a liar, a thief and, yes, she was a murderer. My murderer.

Having lived with two women whose emotions were worn not only on their sleeves, but every part of them, I had shied away from displaying my own. It seemed to me that they had quite enough without me adding to the mix. I thought that my energies would be better focused on more practical things. I now knew for certain that I was wrong. I needed to use every emotion I was feeling to bring this terrible woman to justice, for me, for Mother and the innocent members of The Seven.

I watched Becky tussle with the last of the packages. Once she was satisfied that there were no more to locate, she sat back on her heels and groaned. Over the sound of the sea and Becky's pained breathing, a car engine chuntered to a halt behind the hut. Instantly she was alert and extinguished the light, grabbed a large bread knife with her left hand and limped to the doors. She pulled them shut and stood back, holding the knife at shoulder height, poised to strike.

# CHAPTER 25

I heard footsteps on the pebbles at the side of the hut and shouted a warning, "Mother! She's behind the door." I expected them to stop, but they kept coming. They couldn't hear me.

The feet stopped on the wooden terrace and Becky raised her knife higher. The door started to open and I put every ounce of fear and rage I had inside me into my hand and swung at the metal camping kettle with all my might. I connected with it and the kettle, heavy with water, flew across the hut and hit Becky on the left ear with a mighty crack.

She yelled and smashed back into the wall, the knife falling from her grasp and the wooden hut shuddered with the impact. She slid to the floor, as Mother and Adam rushed inside.

"Becky, what the frigg?" Adam said, illuminating the room with his harsh phone torch as she slumped unconscious onto her side.

"Howard?" Mother whispered into the air.

"I'm here. I'm getting the hang of this thing now," I said, in triumph. It would appear that emotions were definitely useful after all.

"Good for you," she said, watching the kettle roll across the floor and come to rest with its new dent uppermost.

"Stop talking to yourself, it's weird," Adam said, crouching beside Becky. "She's out cold."

"She was getting wads of cash out of the floor," I said. "Her Emergency Parachute, I imagine, to see her safely on the run."

Mother gave a low whistle as she picked up one of the packets, "There has to hundreds of pounds in this one and there are dozens of them."

"Don't touch it," Adam shouted, slapping the packet sharply from her hand. "I mean... finger prints, DNA. The cops'll wanna do forensics and stuff."

"Oh yes, of course," Mother said. "Now what?"

Adam shrugged, as Mother's pink kitty phone began to ring. It took a frantic search through her tote bag to locate it, "Hello?... Yes... Yes... right. We're on our way." She switched it off and tossed it back into the bag. "That was Destiny. We have to go."

Adam looked up, "Why? What's going on?"

Mother held out her hand, "No time to explain, Adam. The car keys, please?"

"Eh?"

"I gave you the keys when we arrived, so I wouldn't lose them."

"Did you?"

"Yes, I did. They'll be in your pockets somewhere."

He began to search his grubby garments, but no sign of the keys, "Don't know where they are," he said with another shrug.

I was ready to grab for the kettle again, exhilarated by the power of my emotion, but Mother was already starting to root through Becky's pockets, "Honestly, just like my husband. Never rely on a man-child," she said.

"What are you doing?" Adam asked.

"Bingo!" Mother said, waving another set of keys in the air. "We're taking the bike."

"I don't think so," I hissed.

"It'll be fine, I've done it before," she said. "Adam, your job is to guard her. Tie her up, knock her out again if you have to. Call 999 and get them out here as quick as you can, let's start the ball rolling. Have you got that?"

Adam looked at Mother, with wide eyes, "K," he said.

She frowned, "He means okay," I explained.

"Why didn't he say so? Come on," and she was off out of the hut. I followed as Adam sank down onto the wooden bench I had been forced to sleep on, clenching and unclenching his fists.

I caught up with Mother on the roadside next to Becky's bike, "Where are we going?"

Mother was wrestling to get Becky's helmet on over her glasses, "Mrs A's on the move. Destiny has followed her to the museum." She forced the helmet on and threw mine to one side, "You won't be needing that."

"I certainly won't, I'm travelling under my own steam."

"Not this time, Harry Potter, I need you to direct me to the museum. I don't know where it is."

"But..."

"Get in, for goodness sake, Howard," she was already clambering aboard.

"But you can't drive one of these things..."

"Says who? Before your father and I met, I was seeing a chap called Rex who had one of these – a Triumph Trident. Beautiful machine. It was fifty years ago, but I'm sure it'll come back."

"But you'll kill yourself," I said, moving round and climbing into the sidecar once again.

"Then I'll be with you forever, won't I," she said, cheerfully.

"That's another very good reason to drive carefully."

She laughed loudly as she revved the engine and swung the bike around in a wild, terrifying loop, "Wagon's roll - one down, one to go!"

Ten minutes later, Destiny was waving at us as Mother drew the motorbike up to the pavement outside Bexhill Museum.

"I'm glad this is nearly over," Mother said, rubbing her knees. "Even I can have too much excitement. I loved that though, took me right back."

I had loved it less and would be picking pieces of hedge out of my hair and clothing if I'd been back in my previous life, such had been the erratic nature of Mother's driving.

"Mrs A left the café and came straight here," Destiny said, looking behind her at the entrance.

"That's fine," Mother said, handing her the helmet. "I only need two minutes with her, before we take her to the police. Is the door locked?"

Destiny shook her head, "No. She had her own set of keys to get in, but she didn't lock the door behind her, I've checked."

"She does the catering here for events," I told Mother.

She pulled her tote bag out of the sidecar and stuck her hand deep inside, "Destiny, stay here. If I'm not out in fifteen minutes call the police."

Destiny gripped her handbag tightly across her tummy, "Are you sure you want to go in alone?"

"I'll be fine, Howard's with me."

"Sue," Destiny said, laying a hand on her shoulder. "I know that's a comfort to you, but in these circumstances I'm not sure his spirit is going to be a lot of help."

"You'd be surprised, he's getting the hang of it. Besides, I've still got this..." she pulled the gun out of her bag and hurried up the stairs to the museum.

"I hope you know what you're doing," Destiny said, as she watched Mother struggling to release her pink dress from the glass door, where she had trapped it behind her.

I was already inside, remembering the foyer from my first visit, "Don't speak, Mum," I said. "We need the element of surprise. Wait here, I'll find her."

She nodded and sat on a padded stool in the shop area, looking very small in the large, dark empty space. I headed into the first gallery, the only lights were the dim emergency ones that gave a sinister quality to the exhibits of rare stuffed birds and dinosaur models. There were stairs in the corner to my right, with a sign pointing down to The Costume and Motoring Galleries and The Wartime Model Railway. There was a large window looking out over Egerton Park and the bright moon lit my way down the stairs to the floor below, but both galleries were dark and silent.

From a far corner I could hear the sounds of scrapes and crashes, as if someone were hurriedly moving boxes or furniture about. I made my way over and stood in front of the grey door of Storeroom 2, or so the sign said on the wall next to it. Light spilled under the door and into the hallway as more muffled sounds of movement emanated from the room.

I turned back to the stairs and quickly went up to the ground floor. I could have just jumped back to Mother, but I was rather pleased with my new found skill at leaping up stairs with ease and indulged myself.

I found her where I had left her, "Mrs A's in the basement. Follow me," I said.

She stood up, "Easier said than done, remember?"

"Oh, yes, well, follow my voice. This way, to the stairs."

We made our way back down, the only sound being the occasional squeak of her plastic sandals on the wooden steps, until we were outside the store room, "She's in here. I heard her shoving things about."

"Stand back then," Mother said, straightening her back and pointing the gun in front of her.

Before I knew it, she had taken a wide stance, leant backwards and kicked out viciously with her right jelly sandal bursting the door open. It flew back and crashed against the shelves behind it. Mrs A screamed and Mother aimed the gun in the very middle of her body, "Don't move or I'll bring you down. I've played darts all my life and you are a bigger bullseye than I'm used to."

Row upon row of metal shelves lined the large storeroom. On them exhibits were boxed or wrapped in white tissue paper, all labelled with tags on strings. It looked very organised and I admired the order of it all, but only briefly when I saw Mrs A on her knees beside a low shelf surrounded by clear plastic boxes that seemed to contain teacups and crockery.

She raised her hands high above her head, "Don't shoot, please. I'm only getting teacups out for a meeting in the morning."

"Really? And what else is down there?" Mother asked

I was ahead of her and got down on my hands and knees to peer into the dark recess at the back of the shelves beside Mrs A, "There's a big pile of plastic wrapped money, like at the beach hut," I reported.

"A plastic pile of big money, wrapped like the beach hut," Mother said. "Or words to that effect. Listen, lady, we know who you are. We know you're Seven, the boss. We have Becky and the police are on their way to her now."

"What? But she said..."

"Yes, she got away from us on the roof, but we found her at the beach hut. She's under guard until the cops arrive. It's all over. Even Carl and Slim have turned on you, they're on their way to the police station too."

"Useless lumps, the pair of them," Mrs A said, spitting the words across the room. "Disgusting creatures. Whatever they say, you have nothing to connect me to any of this. Just because I'm Slim's step-mother, doesn't mean I had anything to do with it. I really don't know what you're talking about."

I stood behind her, "Becky must have called her tonight to let her know they needed to get away."

Mother nodded, "Yes, Becky must have told you she survived the fall off the roof and you needed to make a run for it. Why else are you here picking up all this cash?"

Mrs A sat back on her heels, clearly thinking of her different options. After a moment, she nodded, as if acknowledging that she had run out of road, "She did call me, but you've got it all wrong, my husband was the mastermind of all this nonsense – the drugs, the blackmail. I love running my café. I don't have anything to do with all that."

"Get her phone, the kitty one," I said. "It'll have all the evidence on it the police need."

Mother took a step forward, the gun not moving from dead centre of its target, "Give me your handbag."

"No. Why?"

"Just hand it over, better still put it on the floor and slide it towards me."

Reluctantly, Mrs A did as she was told and soon the blue leather bag was at Mother's feet. She bent down, keeping her eyes on Mrs A for as long as possible before unzipping the bag and tipping its contents onto the floor.

"It's not here," she said, straightening up. "Where is it? The pink kitty phone everyone uses in The Seven?"

"I don't have one," Mrs A said. "Never have. I told you, I just run the café and store some money here for them, that's it. Honestly, Mrs H, it has nothing to do with me."

She reached out nervously towards her belongings.

"Hang on," I said, a small itch starting at the back of my head. Perhaps Henderson's Niggle was still operating. "There's something about the way she said that... 'Mrs H'... wait a minute," I stepped closer to Mrs A, looking closely at her face, as a memory stirred in a distant corner of my brain. "Has she got any identification? Anything with her name on it?"

"What ID have you got?" Mother said, crouching down over the items on the floor.

Mrs A lunged forward, "None, nothing..."

Mother pointed the gun at the ceiling and fired. In the cramped space the shot sounded like a full twenty-one-gun salute. Mrs A screamed again and scrabbled backwards against the wall.

The final piece of the jigsaw fell into place as Mother turned over a driving license and I was able to read the name.

"Hazel," I said, staring at my childhood friend.

"Hazel? Not Hazel Richardson?" Mother said, her eyes wide. "But she died..."

"Hello, Mrs H," Hazel said, with a weak smile, patting the conker-coloured curls of what I could now see was her dyed hair.

"Yes - Mrs H - that's what you used to call me when you rang to talk to Howard."

We were interrupted by the sound of heavy feet pounding down the stairs and Destiny burst in behind us, brandishing a huge dinosaur bone pulled, I imagine, from a display upstairs.

"It's alright, Destiny, I'm okay," Mother said. "Stand down. Just a warning shot, for this one, who's about to tell us where she's been all these years. Meet Becky's long dead mother, Hazel Richardson."

# CHAPTER 26

Hazel's shoulders sank as she slumped against the wall, "I'm really sorry about Howard, he wasn't supposed to be harmed. You have to believe me, he was my friend. Becky got frustrated and a bit carried away."

Mother shook her head, "A *bit*? It might have been Becky who killed him, but you were doing your best to steal his money, weren't you? So don't you dare say he was your *friend*," she said, her anger spiking. "Just tell me how this all happened."

"Oh, dear. Well, Tony, my late husband, always had some sort of scheme or racket going. Before he died, he got a solicitor on-side, Simon Moon his name is. He feeds us tips about clients of his we could use or scam. About a month ago, he told us about this chap who was going to die of cancer quite soon and was sorting out his estate. Nearly a million pounds going begging, he said. No real family to leave it to, just his elderly mother – no offence, Mrs H.

When he told me the client's name was Howard Henderson, I wondered if it was the same Howard I knew as a child in Rye – and I couldn't believe it when it was. But I hadn't seen him in years, since I got pregnant with Becky and ran off. That's when they came up with the idea; tell Howard I'd died and that Becky is his daughter, then get her to inherit everything. From what Simon said, Howard didn't have long to live and was thinking about refusing any treatment, so it wouldn't take long.

The plan was for them to get Howard all mixed up in the group. They called it The Seven to make it sound grander than it was. It's just a small-time drugs operation really, plus the odd dog and car theft if they can be bothered. The money from Howard would have been the biggest hustle they've ever done. At first, they didn't want all his money, just some of it, but he got greedy..."

"He? Doesn't she mean she? Becky?" I said.

"Who are you talking about? If you're not the kingpin... or queenpin, this had to be Becky's idea," Mother said.

"Not really, she was keen on it when he suggested it, but he's the brains behind it all."

Mother nodded, "Dave Ellis, the policeman? I knew he was involved."

"Dave?" Hazel said. "No, he's nothing to do with it. He was just my husband's dopey friend. I know he doesn't look much, but Adam's the boss. He runs it all."

I was sure I'd misheard her, "Adam?"

"Adam?" Mother repeated. "Scrawny little Adam? No, that can't be right."

"Yes, how else do you think he knew about everyone's problems for the blackmail? He's brilliant at all that IT stuff, hacking police files, court documents, insurance files, drugs manifests, all sorts."

Destiny stepped forward, "So, he wasn't being

blackmailed at all?"

"No sister in politics?" Mother said.

"No, nothing like that. Him and Becky have been an item for a few years. When my Tony died, Adam took over. He's brighter than he looks."

"No wonder he knew what everyone was saying in their kitty phone messages," I said. "They were all texting *him*! It was all upside down, no wonder he kept the first phone, Becky even said it – he was Number One. The boss. We were looking in the wrong direction for Seven; he had both phones all the time."

Destiny looked nervously at Mother, "I think it's time to call the police, don't you?"

Mother turned to her, "Are you ready? You'll have a lot of explaining to do to your husband."

"I know, but at least I have a chance of fighting to keep him, unlike you and Henderson. Either way, like you said, I'll survive. I'll have to for my son's sake."

"It's a boy?"

Destiny nodded, "Yes."

Hazel shuffled forward on her knees, "Please, you have to believe me, I didn't want Howard dead. I liked him. It was lovely to see him again."

Mother gave her a withering look, "Tell that to the police."

"Sue?" Destiny said. "Where's Adam now?"

I started, "Good lord!"

"Christ on a bike, we left him to guard Becky and call the police," Mother shouted. "Destiny, stay here and look after Hazel. Hand her over when the police get here, bash her with that old bone if she misbehaves."

She ran for the stairs, "If my knees make it to the top, I'll be very surprised," she panted, with me hot on her tail. The sound of a door banging above stopped us on the third step.

"Who's that? Mother, stay still."

I tiptoed up the stairs - not that my tread would have disturbed anyone - and peered around a pillar to see Adam and a limping Becky creeping slowly across the gallery.

Becky carried her large rucksack again, stuffed with her emergency money, I assumed. Adam carried a gun.

I turned to Mother, "Get back into the store room. It's Adam, he's got a..."

"Oy! Stay put, old woman," Adam yelled, from behind us.

Mother dived into her bag to get her gun out again, but Adam was too quick for her with his long skinny legs. He leapt down the stairs and snatched the bag from her, "I think one friggin' gun is enough, don't you?"

"Mum? Where are you?" Becky shouted, as she hobbled down the stairs behind Adam, her face now a mass of bruises and dried blood.

"In the storeroom," Hazel shouted back. "There's another one in here... oof!" There was a hefty thump, which I assumed meant that Destiny's dinosaur bone had hit its target.

"Come on, old woman," Adam said, leading her down the stairs.

I walked beside them back into the storeroom, "Hang on, Mother, I'll think of something."

"I know you will Henderson. You're a problem solver, your dad always said that..."

"Shut up, with all this talking to no one crap," Adam said, jamming the gun into her back. "Get inside." He pushed her roughly through the door.

Destiny was standing holding the bone, while Hazel sat at her feet rubbing her shoulder.

"What the frigg? Put it down and get back against the wall," Adam gestured with his gun to the far end of the storeroom. "You too, old woman."

Destiny hesitated, but Mother nodded at her and she put down her prehistoric weapon and moved to the wall. I stayed put beside Adam, who had now been joined by a dazed looking Becky.

"Got the cash?" Adam asked Hazel.

"Getting it now, love," she said. "I was just sorting it out when this lot charged in. What a lot of fuss? Honestly, Becky, if you hadn't been so hot headed..."

"Shut up, Mum, just get the rest of the money."

Mother tutted, "I had to tell Slim off about speaking badly about his mother, earlier. I think you and I are going to be having words soon, too, young Rebecca."

"Don't call me that," Becky shouted, flinching as the noise and movement caused pain from her injuries. "My name is Becky," she mumbled.

Mother took a step towards Becky, "I think I'll call you whatever I like. You murdered my son, and you and your skinny little rag-man here can't do anything worse to me than you've already done."

"Wait," I said, as Adam pointed his gun sharply at her.

"Back the frigg off, old woman."

Mother hesitated then stepped back beside Destiny. Hazel was pulling out bags of money from the back of the shelf and stuffing them into a holdall beside her. Adam stood nervously in the centre of the room, the gun twitching in his hand.

My options were limited, but I had to do something, so I moved as close to Becky as I could without actually touching her. She flinched and shivered, "Did you feel that? It went really cold; it's like this damn place is haunted."

Bingo, that was it. I knew what to do.

"Mother, don't say anything yet, but I want you to repeat everything I say. Don't wait, don't change the words. Say it exactly as I say it, whatever happens. Do you understand?"

"Yes, Howard."

Becky stared at Mother, "Why did she say Howard?"

Adam shrugged, "She's been doing it all night. Thinks she's talking to him. She's lost her marbles, ignore her."

I stepped close to Becky again, she shivered and spun around, "The Seagull has landed," I said and Mother repeated the phrase.

Becky swung back to Mother, "W-what did you say?"

"You heard," I said and closed in on her to make her shiver again.

"You heard," Mother said.

"Do seagulls ever sleep, or do they just cry salt tears?" Mother repeated my words exactly as I had spoken them, getting the hang of what I was doing.

"Stop that, STOP IT," Becky yelled, pointing at Mother, yelping with pain as she grasped her broken arm. She then shivered and jumped away as I got as close as I could to her again.

"Do you want me to do Riverdance over the pebbles again?" Mother asked, echoing my words.

"Adz, make her stop. Why is she saying that?" Becky screamed, but he just looked at her as if she'd gone mad.

"Calm down," he said. "What the frigg, Becky? She's just trying to wind you up."

"No, no, you don't understand. *He* did the Riverdance. *Henderson*. He couldn't walk on the stupid beach, it's what I said to him."

"Maybe you'll finally get time to read that Barbara Cartland book, where you're going."

"No, NO. Adam, listen, we talked about the book under my chair leg, *him* and me - it's by Barbara Cartland. She wouldn't know that."

"I trusted you, Becky. I bought you an ice cream, red sauce for you, none for me. You made me expose myself to a dog walker."

"The spaniel woman," she gasped, as she began to stagger around the room, looking for the voice that was feeding Mother. "I didn't make you strip off. I didn't. It was Adam, he thought it was funny."

"You didn't have to kill me, Becky."

She crashed into a shelf, screaming with the pain from her arm, "Stop it, stop it."

"I should have given you some money, I didn't handle that very well. I apologise."

"Go away..."

"You held my hand at the Sunnyside Guest House, you were kind to me. But you lied, Becky. You really should have been an actress. You're a good liar. Your mum shouldn't have stopped your childhood dream."

"What?" Hazel said, staring at Mother. "How did you know that?"

"Make her stop... make HIM stop!" Becky was yelling as she threw herself at Adam and snatched the gun. She waved it wildly around her, spinning round and round trying to see where I was.

"There, there, Becky. No more killing, you know I'm not very good at comforting people."

"Shut up," Becky shouted. "Shush..." and the gun exploded with a flash and boom. Everyone ducked and fell to the floor. She spun again, "Go away, Henderson. You're dead, you're DEAD."

Boom! The gun fired for a second time, to the sounds of screams and yells from those on the floor.

Suddenly, Adam rose and lunged at Becky, knocking the gun from her hand. It flew past me and skidded under the bottom shelf by the door. Adam flung himself onto the floor and tried to reach it, just as Mother got to her feet – quite calmly, I thought – and walked two steps to the middle of the room carrying the large dinosaur bone she had picked up from where Destiny had dropped it. Like a baseball player hitting a home run, she swung the ancient bone through the air with a hiss and knocked Becky clean off her feet. She went down without a sound and didn't move.

Mother stood for a moment, the bone hanging limply by her side, then, as if every ounce of energy left her body at the same moment, she sank gently to her knees and began to cry. Destiny crawled across the floor to her and wrapped her in her arms.

I stepped over Becky to Hazel, who was laying on her side groaning quietly. She was holding her hip tightly and through her fingers I could see blood running from a wound. One of Becky's gun shots must have hit her. It didn't look life threatening, but she wouldn't be going anywhere in a hurry.

I heard the squeaking of trainers on a rubber floor behind me and turned to see Adam's back disappearing out of the door. The window onto Egerton Park popped into my mind and I was suddenly at the top of the stairs looking down on him as he pounded towards me.

"Bingo!" I shouted, as I swept six beautifully displayed Japanese silk kimonos off their hooks beside me in one smooth movement. They flew down around him and got twisted up with his feet. He stumbled back a couple of steps and then rolled with a thud to the bottom of the stairs.

I followed him as he kicked his legs free and scooted back across the corridor, taking off around the corner. I continued my pursuit and we found ourselves in an especially dark, unlit area of the museum. Adam looked about him for a means of escape and saw a dimly lit exit sign above a fire door in the far corner. He dashed towards it and slammed into it, but it wouldn't open. He shoved it again with all his scrawny might, but it wouldn't budge.

He thumped the door, until the sound of a tinny hoot made him freeze. Through the silence came another little hoot, followed by the gentle chug of a steam train. He turned, terror in his eyes, as he saw that the opposite corner of the room had come to life. Tiny houses glowed through the darkness with illuminated windows. Centimetres high streetlamps glimmered in the dark. Children were frozen in a snowball fight, ladies held in suspended animation as they gossiped outside a greengrocer's shop. The snow on the roof of a miniature De La Warr Pavilion glistened as an old steam engine chugged and wobbled its way around the town on its tiny gauge track.

"What the frigg'?" Adam whispered and staggered towards the train set. Luckily, the remembered joy of such happy times with my childhood passion, had allowed me to flick the switches and bring this beautiful model railway to life.

As he drew close, I looked into his eyes. This odious youth who had brought so much misery to people. Who had used their past wrongs to further his petty crimes and miserable schemes. Who had made me drop my trousers and expose my doughy flesh for his amusement in the middle of the park.

I reached out and swung the large metal door beside me at him with all my might. It hit him on the back of the shoulder and propelled him cleanly into the mock-up of a war-time air raid shelter. The door slammed and

I used my remaining anger towards him to ram the bolt home. He hammered on the door of the first of many cells he would be experiencing in the long days and months ahead.

I watched the miniature train circle the perfectly recreated town of Bexhill-On-Sea during war-time. The gentle sound of its wheels on the track were soothing and blended with the wail of sirens in the distance. I found I was able to straighten a tree that had fallen over in Egerton Park, close to the pond. I flicked some pebbles out of the blue painted sea. A miniscule seagull had slipped from its place on the top of a yellow beach hut and I gently placed him back on top. Everything looked neat and orderly. Everything was in its place, as the sound of a distant flute blew across the room.

# EPILOGUE

The familiar avenue of horse chestnut trees stretches up the slope in front of me. The ground falls away to my right down to the field that doubles as the local cricket pitch. The summer sun warms my neck and yet I have to foxtrot around conkers wrapped in their spiky autumn jackets, while being careful not to trample delicate snowdrops. The seasons seem irrelevant here, with their best parts existing all at once.

Behind me is the little Sussex village and stone church of Jevington. I know it well; Maggie's service was held there. Mine too. I didn't go, it didn't seem appropriate really. I left them all to grieve for me in their own way. Funerals are for the living after all.

I'm not certain how I got here. The warm breeze seemed to lift me up and hold me, until it brought me here. What I am certain of is that if I go over the hill in front of me, I will see Maggie again. How do I know she's there, waiting for me? Heaven knows, is the best answer I can give for now. She will be in her Strawberry Thief deckchair – always on the right. My chair was always on the left. She'll hold out the flask suggesting I pour more tea and ask if I've eaten all the egg sandwiches. I never have, I always make sure I save the last one for her.

I contemplate picking up some conkers and putting them in my pocket for her. Mother used to paint faces on them, she said it was fun. It didn't feel very funny when their heads split open as you swung them at your opponent's, their eyes and noses cracking. I understand now that she meant well, with her fun.

Mother has many friends who all want to look after her. She also has Destiny now and a blossoming friendship with Carl and Slim. They'll all be okay, in time.

I shake my head and smooth my hands down my cream linen jacket, no longer crumpled from the rough and tumble of recent days, and I think of the tale I have to tell Maggie.

Shooting a man – all be it by mistake. Being both hunted and hunter. Finding and losing a family. Shinning up walls, riding motorbikes, falling from cliffs, exposing myself in the park, washing in buckets, urinating in the sea... I may skim over that part. But she'll want me to tell it properly, all of it. I'll have to tell her that I was fooled by Becky, that I made myself gullible, that I had wanted to die – she'll shake her head, tut a bit, but I know she'll be proud of me for catching them all in the end.

Becky is going away for a long time. They're all vying to lay the blame at each other's door, but they'll get their just punishments. It seems such a waste of so many lives. I know my life was wasted too, but I was ready to go, to move on. Is it odd that I actually feel I've gained so much more than them?

Right, Maggie awaits. Onwards.

Why do I hesitate? I've dreamt of her here on the

Sussex Downs in our usual spot ever since she went. I know now that those dreams were real or as real as anything is where I am, but I feel different. I am different.

My time without her has changed me, brought out things that my life with her never did. Oh, I wouldn't change anything. Twenty-five years together can't be undone, and I wouldn't choose to do so, but that was then. That was old Henderson, Maggie's Henderson, the upholsterer. I am the new Henderson. My Henderson; the family man, the sleuth... The Seagull.

I'm not sure I'm the man she married anymore. Will she still love me?

A seagull - *my* seagull, glides through the blue sky overhead, encouraging me onwards and I keep walking, the ground rising gently ahead of me. I crest the hill and she's there. Not sitting in her deckchair, but standing facing me. She smiles. I'd forgotten what it was like, her smile. Uninhibited, loving, magnificent.

"The seagull is here," she says.

"I am... I mean, how did you know?"

She steps aside and there is my seagull settled on the grass feasting on egg sandwiches. It stops and looks at me, nods, then launches itself into the air with a triangle of bread held in its beak. We watch as the wide wings pivot and tilt to catch the breeze, before sailing away across the downs.

"I am The Seagull," I say, as I turn to Maggie.

"Are you? Well, that needs some thinking about."

"And I'm happy."

She smiles again and sits in her Strawberry Thief

deckchair, "Good, it's about time. Now, sit down and tell me everything."

I sit in my usual chair, on the left, and watch her reach down for the flask of tea, "It's hard to know where to begin, so much has happened. Let's see, I can list the main events;

Monday, two letters arrived,

Tuesday, I became a father,

Wednesday, I was on the run.

Thursday, I fell to my death.

Friday, I caught my killer.

It's been quite a week."

# THANK YOU

Thank you for reading Death and The Seagull.

If you enjoyed the book, please review it on Amazon.co.uk so other readers can follow Henderson's adventures in Bexhill.

If you have been searching for the tribute to Agatha Christie's ABC Murders hidden within this book, the solution is as follows:

The first three members of The Seven are Adam (Number 1), Becky (Number 2) and Callum (Number 3).

They are A. B. C.

# OTHER BOOKS

## *by Mark Feakins*

**The Rye Series:**

#1 The Rye Rooftop Club: The Great British Romcom.

#2 The Rye Rooftop Club: Mother's Day

**Other stand-alone books:**

Death & The Seagull

**Coming soon:**

#3 The Rye Rooftop Club: Summer Solstice

All available on Amazon.co.uk

# ACKNOWLEDGEMENTS

Thanks again to all of my friends and acquaintances who have had their names recycled for this book. Although I have borrowed their names, I have not used any of their characteristics, and any peculiarities of the characters named after them are entirely of my own creation.

Thanks also to my key early readers, Andy Hawkins (you can get on with writing your own book now) & Martin Scattergood (AKA T'husband) for their continued enthusiasm, guidance and keen eye for errors and plot holes.

Thanks to Bexhill Museum for providing such a great venue for key parts of this story, and apologies for messing around with the layout of the different galleries and storerooms to fit my needs. For anyone reading this far, Bexhill Museum really is a great place to visit with a brilliant costume gallery, dinosaurs and the most beautiful Winter Wartime Model Railway.

www.bexhillmuseum.org.uk

Finally, thanks to our beautiful, gentle, chubby, ginger cat, Henderson, for lending me his name for this book.

# ABOUT THE AUTHOR

Mark Feakins grew up on the Sussex coast and lived in Bexhill-On-Sea during the heady days of his youth, in the 1970's and 1980's. He then moved to London to go to drama school and, after a brief time as an actor, ran a number of high-profile theatres. He then travelled north as Executive Producer of Sheffield Theatres before creating his own photography business. He has a degree in Librarianship, danced around a maypole on BBC TV's Playschool and won Channel 4's Come Dine with Me in 2010.

Mark now lives happily in the region of Valencia in Spain, with his husband Martin.

His family still live in Bexhill-On-Sea and his mother, Beryl, is regularly to be found behind the counter of Bexhill Museum. Please go and say, Hello!

E: markfeakins@gmail.com

Facebook: My Writing Life

Printed in Great Britain
by Amazon

32511052R00160